The Avenger's Wild Boar Hunt

Norena   Soumakis

A peculiar virtue in wildlife ethics is that the hunter ordinarily has no gallery to applaud or disapprove of his conduct. Whatever his acts, they are dictated by his own conscience, rather than a mob of onlookers. It is difficult to exaggerate the importance of this fact.
_____Aldo Leopold

Other Books by the Author

Going Against Traffic

Murder at the Foul Fowl Farm

Murder at Valtaki Cove

Murder at the Olive Oil Factory

The Greek Graffiti Murders

Chapter 1

"Did I hear you correctly? One friend shot the other in the back?" Geró Peerooney motioned his partner Pidalios to silence as he tried to hear Captain Sakalidis.

"That's what I said—happened up here on Mt. Tayegatos. They were hunting wild boar. One man is dead, and the friend is beside himself with grief. He called it in on his own phone."

"So, it was an accident?"

"Probably, hunters are shot by other hunters occasionally, but this one—I don't know, it's not sitting right with me: time of call, scene, no witnesses. Could you and Pidalios come up while the scene is new. I don't want other people or wild animals tainting evidence. Today is the opening day of hunting season, and I only have Sgt. Goovis and the doctor with me. I value your opinions."

"John, compliments always work. You just got your consultants." Geró guffawed. "My nephew is here with me now. I'll fill him in and make a quick stop at home. I was supposed to take Irini to dinner. Tell me exactly where you are up there, and we'll arrive as quickly as we can."

Geró hung up, gave Pidalios the scrap of paper that he had written the mountain location on and explained the scant details the captain had related. His nephew responded, "We filed our last case as 'Mystery at the Foul Fowl Farm.' We're graduating to wild boar hunts, a step up, I'd say. At least these animals are bigger and scarier than chickens."

His uncle, giving him a sidelong glance, said, "All right, comedian, if you can get the car, I'll be right down." Pidalios still drove his old 335 BMW coupe, and the pampered silver beauty was sparkling in the Greek November sunshine when Geró came downstairs. Pidalios drove to Leonidou 53 and sat in his uncle's back parking lot space to wait. He called his Thia Irini to tell her to buzz her husband in and inquired as to her well being today. These two first met on the telephone before his uncle married Irini many years ago. His aunt had become not only a relative but also a close friend since she arrived in Sparta from New York City.

Back then his name "Pidalios?" was spoken tentatively by her so soon after her marriage to his uncle.

"It's so nice to speak with you, Thia mou."

"Does that mean my aunt?"

"It certainly does; welcome to our family. I am looking forward to meeting the woman who married my favorite uncle and partner."

"Thank you for that. He tells me you and your brother Dimitri are going to be my favorite relatives."

"My Thio is always right."

"In other words I am Thia, and he is Thio—with an 0, right?"

"You are a fast learner." His warm laughter endeared him to her.

"It is a pleasure to know you," she said.

"The pleasure is all mine, and I look forward to meeting you in person, Thia."

She said goodbye, turned to her new husband and said, "Geró, he understood me; he speaks perfect English!"

"He lived in Toronto, Canada, until he was eleven. He's my nephew, so he's smart."

He told Irini that the Pidalion was an 1800s modern Greek book on Canon law. St. Nicodemus of the Holy Mountain in the Pidalion: "invokes the double standard of strictness and exactness in the household and the family. Thus, these are the ways of the spirit and the steerer, the guide to salvation— Pidalios."

Geró was buzzed in by Irini, as if she knew he had arrived at the downstairs door. As it was her thirty year habit, she waited for the sound of the elevator and held the door open to their apartment. Besides writing important things on small scraps of paper, he always forgot his keys. "Irinimou, it's as if you know the exact moment I'm coming up. How do you do that?"

"That's the Μοεραε," [the more ay—the Fates in Ancient Greece] she sang happily and said, "just as Dean Martin's song was meant to be sung."

"You're just showing off your ever-increasing knowledge of Greek," he teased. "Pidalios called you, right?"

"I confess."

"Good, because now you can forgive me. I know I promised dinner at Valtaki Cove, but sadly a call from the Astynomia (Greek police) to come to a death scene will have to take precedence over a pleasant evening with my wife."

"That's kind of you to say, but the real reason you came up was to get a jacket." She opened the closet. "One for you and one for my nephew. It gets chilly at night up there."

Almost as an aside he said, "This woman, she buzzes me in, reminds me of important dates coming up, loves my family, learned Greek, and she is still good looking."

"No ass kissing, you faker; take the jackets and go. Be careful, and I'll wait to hear the details."

He threw the coats over his arm, kissed her cheek, and she heard him say, as he walked away, "and she'll wait up, not for me, but to get information for a possible next mystery novel."

Pidalios drove Geró through Sparta and onto Gytheio Road, the six kilometers to the turn off for the village of Xerokambe, the road to Kaminia, seamlessly leading from one to the next through live trees that had just given up their fruit to the local owners and all the seasonal foreign hired help. Olive picking was hard work that used to be done by village men, their wives and families. Now the trees stood stripped until the next crop. Greek olives were pressed between giant stones turned by mules decades ago to get the oil. Those who still owned many acres took their harvest to local olive oil factories for the magnificent deep green oil to be pressed and canned by machines. Greece provided eighty percent of the world's olive oil. Some other countries bought large quantities, blended it with their own and called it pure.

"When the olive oil museum opened just a few streets from our apartment," Geró said, "Thia was the perfect visitor. She got there very early and waited outside—reading a book, of course." He smiled at the memory.

"There wasn't much doing in Sparta for a cultured woman then," Pidalios winked. "No wonder she smoked those long brown More cigarettes. She was bored, right?"

"But she stopped nineteen years ago. Maybe, if you went to a museum or two, you would finally quit too."

"Always a comeback," Pidalios said as he turned his full attention to driving up the twisting mountain road. His left hand held his lit cigarette up to the slightly open window.

He knew the narrow road up Mt. Tayegatos—the sharp ess curves, so treacherous, that one driver would blow his horn before attempting a blind curve. The possibility of another oncoming car was always a danger. Pidalios called Capt. Sakalidis to inform him of their imminent arrival, and he backed onto a gravel, off-road path, overlooking the ravine where the shooting had occurred earlier. "Do you want to hold my arm, old man?" he kidded Geró as they descended to the crime scene below.

"Αστηέβεσε?" [as tee ev esse-Are you joking?]

Pidalios felt comfortable with the verbal swipe, even though his uncle was on the wrong side of middle age. Geró was a very strong older man in such excellent shape that no one could keep up with the rapid pace at which he walked. His speed was legendary, and his mental acuity was well beyond other men his age.

Both men had been police officers in the Astynomia until Geró, an oft-decorated detective in the department, tired of the breakdown in standards and growing corruption. These determined his decision to quit. Pidalios had followed within a year of tolerating another economic crisis in Greece. This caused the loss of local laboratory facilities, fewer officers, modern weaponry and vests. New technologies and their own personal phones were helpful, but the set, incompetent leadership and 'job for life' attitude, created by government bureaucracy, was the final straw.

Together the two relatives opened a private agency in Sparta. A simple brass plaque at the door to their small office on the second floor simply said: detective agency. They had to begin with minor cases, but their positive reputation, and Geró's bringing clients after he solved the murder of his former department chief, increased business. The two men were excellent detectives, and the police heads in Athens saved on budget money by hiring them on a case by case needs basis. The new man in charge of their old department, Capt. John Sakalidis, still short staffed, had called on them today. Geró and Pidalios walked carefully down the narrow, rocky pathway to the scene and acknowledged John and Sgt. Dimitri Goovis.

The captain began. "The deceased is Vrasithas Politis. It appears that he was shot in the back with a shotgun, fired by Fotis Grigoris, that man sitting over there under that tree." They all glanced at him, sitting curled with knees bent up to support his head in his hands. "We'll speak to him in a minute," Sakalidis continued. "He said his friend Politis was walking a few paces ahead of him, tracking a wild boar. Grigoris followed quietly behind, gun at the ready. Accidentally, according to him, he shot and killed his friend. When he realized Politis was dead, it took him some time to regain his senses, he told me. Then he called us. I brought Dr. Karis from Sparta up with the sergeant and me. You guys know each other."

After listening and noting the sweep of the scene, Geró and Pidalios were shown the positive identification of the dead man from items found in his pockets. Pidalios took down his home address. "Was he married?"

"Yes, his wife's name is Katina. He had two small boys, and they live in Kaminia."

Dr. Harilaos Karis was getting something from the trunk of the police cruiser and talking on his cell phone. Then, wearing gloves, he didn't shake hands but offered a business-like greeting. Earlier he had asked the captain to call for an army helicopter from the base on Gytheio Rd. "We can't take him out of this gulch in a car. The helicopter can lower a basket. Here, help me zip him into the bag. Careful, Sgt. Goovis. He may be dead but he still has much to tell us. Until I can do a post mortem at Sparta Nosokomeio [hospital], I can only tell you he was shot in the back, and that seems to be the cause of death. More later." The cops assisted the doctor, and, as they heard the sound of an approaching copter, Dr. Karis said he would accompany the body back to Sparta.

"Not a very friendly guy," said Pidalios as the door closed, and the doctor waited inside to take off on board with the 'cargo.'

"Let's talk to Grigoris," said John. "When we first came, he was very emotional over killing his friend—wailing, crying. We secured the area, and in that time he seems to have calmed down."

"When you called, you said something was odd. Anything to add?" Geró asked his friend.

"You're a detective. You know. It's that feeling in your gut. I saw something…."

"It always comes back," Geró reassured him. "If it wakes you up tonight, write it down so you remember in the morning." He laughed.

"You're right about that, my friend. Pidalios is near Grigoris. Let's walk over."

Pidalios walked back toward them. "I know this guy, Fotis Grigoris. I've seen him around the horios (villages), from Kaminia, I think. I never heard he was ever in trouble—case closed?"

Geró froze his nephew with a look. "'Quod gratis asseritur: gratis negator.'"

"He has that Latin phrase on the wall in our office, captain," Pidalios responded to his quizzical look. "It means: what can be asserted without evidence can be dismissed without evidence."

"Maybe I'll get a copy of that for my office." The head of dark brown hair with touches of grey lifted to look at them as they approached him, sitting by a black pine tree.

"Σηλητητίρια [see lee pee teria-condolences]. We understand you are grieving over your friend but you know that there are questions we must ask."

His dirty face displayed tear tracks from his still watery eyes. "Why?" He cried out. "He was my friend, and I killed him. I admit it, okay? It was an accident. There is nothing I can say to bring him back."

"We realize all that," Sakalidis said, but it is a police investigation. You have to tell us all you can remember. This gentleman is former senior detective, Geró Peerooney, and his partner Pidalios, also a detective. They are here to help. We want to put this down as accidental death, but you have to tell us step by step from when you got here. Do you need another moment to calm yourself? If not, please begin."

"The beginning is also the end. I shot him, and that's all."

"Did you intend to do it?" Sakalidis asked.

"Of course not!" he bellowed.

"Then just tell us the events leading up to and including the shooting." The captain was impatient.

"Okay, okay. We came here. We were excited because of hunting season starting today, November 1. We wanted a wild boar. Then…"

"Then what? C'mon, help us here," said Pidalios.

"I tripped—lot of vines and rocks up here. A shot rang out, and the next thing I know I'm on my belly, Vras is down, blood splattered, just horrible." He put his head down, and the extent of his suffering was obvious in his heaving back. They waited and waited.

"Fotis?"

"Everyone calls me Fo," he responded, sounding annoyed.

"Okay, Fo," John repeated. We are losing light. The helicopter is hovering, and they must take the doctor and your friend to Sparta. Let's all walk over to the car. You'll be more comfortable there."

"So, you're arresting me?"

"No, we are going to the station to complete your statement. Sgt. Goovis and Pidalios are staying behind to bag evidence to back up your story."

"It's no story. It's the truth!" He was very agitated now.

"Look, I'm hungry; you need food and shelter, and the detectives want to wrap this up. You can eat while you answer our questions. Let's go."

Name Day Celebration in Greece

Chapter 2

Captain Sakalidis carefully protected the top of Fotis Grigoris' head as he helped him into the back seat of the police cruiser headed to Astynomia headquarters on Επιςκοπου Βρεςθενεs (Episkopou Vresthenes) in Sparta. He gave the gun, belonging to Fotis, to one of the others to lock up. Pidalios stayed with Sgt. Goovis on Mt. Tayegatos. Once again they checked the immediate area of death, the surrounding flora and sparse forest of black pines. Cypress, junipers, oak and evergreen grew hit or miss on the sides of the ravine.

Items bagged into evidence were few. They found slugs to be kept for possible fingerprints. These were some distance from the Remington Vrasithas Politis had held. Very carefully they wrapped and saved his gun. Another single shell directly and far ahead of where the body fell was probably from an involuntary reaction of pulling the trigger when his body lurched forward after being hit. Twigs and thick vines, which Grigoris claimed he tripped over, were dug out of the ground and bagged. All of this would probably lead nowhere. It was associative evidence, as was the empty aluminum foil-lined found packet of Fisherman's Friend cough drops. "Terrible tasting," Pidalios grimaced, "but quite effective." Saliva and prints might be obtained from the small box or the foil wrapping crammed inside it. There was also a long clump of dark brown hair, probably human, caught on a pine cone.

Some of the bloodstained soil up there by a track was probably animal blood, Pidalios thought, but he dutifully scraped some with the soil into a plastic bag—an evidence bag. He always carried a variety of sizes in his pocket. He was caught in the remembrance of the first case he worked on with his Thio Geró, and Pidalios was asked for just such a bag. When he replied that he hadn't brought any, his uncle lectured him on their importance at any crime scene. He never forgot them again.

After a post midnight rain, the muddy grasses were stuck in another deep shoe print. It was also molded, cast and bagged. Oddly, this print was facing downward on the side of the hill.

So many anxious opening day hunters had been camping out in the area since before dawn. Scattered among them would have been a few cruel, trigger-happy people, always known to shoot at anything that moved. Along with dead birds, squirrels and foxes, shot for kicks and left behind, a fellow hunter had once been accidentally shot. Luckily, he survived. The game wardens were always frustrated in their search for the mentally disturbed or abusive type of man or woman. Tourists hunted and then went home, and some of these big game, international hunting types ignored all rules.

While Sgt. Goovis checked for other usable clues, Pidalios, climbing up and down both side of the hills, came upon an unusual object: a red hair ribbon still tied in a perfect bow, attached to a limb. It appeared to have been placed there, but that was doubtful. Agreeing their search was complete, he and Goovis untied the crime scene tape, pulled up the metal boundary stakes and cones, took all the evidence bags and climbed to where Pidalios had parked. They put all their outer garb into the trunk and drove off after they checked that nothing had been left behind.

Crime and accidental death scenes are always checked with utmost care in modern policing. The concept, known as Locard's Exchange Principle, is that, when someone enters or leaves a scene, something physical is either brought in by that person or taken out of the area. Thus, it is the reason for often wearing net caps, booties, step-in sanitized coveralls, masks and plastic gloves. By adhering to Locard's theory, many answers are found, and people are either linked to a crime, or the death is declared otherwise, such as murder, by the coroner.

———————

An overwrought Fotis Grigoris picked up the burger and checked for ketchup. "Alati and peppiri [salt and pepper] is already on here? Thanks for the food, even though I don't really feel hungry; you understand, don't you, that I need something. I ate only jerky and coffee up there at dawn before we started. Μαλακά [asshole], he hit himself in the forehead. Did anyone find my thermos?" After expressing concern over his misplaced property, he picked up a Sprite and, taking a big swallow, lowered his eyes. "I can't believe it. I shot my good friend."

"You get yourself together while I begin the tape," said Sakalidis. "This is Captain John Sakalidis of Sparta Astynomia. It is 6:06 pm, November 1,1995. Fotis Grigoris has been advised of his rights in connection with this morning's shooting death of Vrasithas Politis, also a resident of Kaminia. He refused counsel and knows his statements are being taped. Also present are private detectives and consultants, Geró Peerooney and Pidalios. Is this correct, Mr. Grigoris?"

A soft but clear voice answered, "Yes."

Looking up at Grigoris John asked, "You and Vrasithas Politis, your friend, were on the mountain to hunt wild boar this morning, were you not?"

"Yes, and we were not just friends,

becoming good friends," Fotis answered in a shaky voice, "ever since he came from Australia—maybe four years ago."

John stopped the tape and said, "Please don't tell a story. We want you to answer briefly, okay?" He started the tape.

Geró asked, "Are you aware of anyone who wanted to harm him, who didn't get along with him?"

"Vras was one of those guys everybody liked." He paused for a moment to swallow some emotion and to blot his eyes with the paper napkin. "He knew he had to be accepted, so…"

"You just said he 'had to be accepted;' why would you say that?" Sakalidis broke in.

"Did I? I meant he wanted so much to be liked in the horio (village). You know, new kid on the block and all that," joked Fotis. "He played the good boy, smiling at all the old ladies, always 'καλί μερα' (kalee mera) in the morning. He volunteered help to neighbors, came to the kafenion and listened to the old men—never interrupting their long, often repeated tales of past history."

"Normal behavior," said Sakalidis.

"Everyone saw him in church at Mass every Sunday with the wife and kids. You know all the gossip in small villages, and Kaminia is very small—so is our church."

"Were you there on those Sundays?" asked Pidalios. "No? So, what you're saying is he was a kind and decent person." Pidalios put an end to Grigoris' ongoing list of positive qualities of the dead friend by saying, "You sound almost envious. We asked you who disliked him?"

Ignoring the sarcasm, he answered, "Honestly, I can't think of a soul—at least not enough for anyone to kill him." The wide, innocent eyes challenged Pidalios.

"But you did," Pidalios took a verbal swipe at him.

"Geró picked up the questioning. "The two of you planned today's hunt. When? a week? a month ago?"

"Why would that matter?"

"If it doesn't, please answer the question."

"Quite a while ago. I always want to go hunting, but it is a dying sport in our village.

My father always talked about it ever since I was a little kid. We would all sit facing the fireplace in our maternal grandparents' hamoukela [traditional, small old stone house], built by my great grandfather. We would eat roasted chestnuts or whatever my mother grilled in the skara [grill basket]—not much else to do in the winter in Kaminia, except use my slingshot to bring down small animals or birds."

"Please get back to answering our questions." John was tired of pausing the tape.

Ignoring the captain, he went on. "Anyhow, my father always told hunting stories, his adventures up on Tayegatos. I guess those are what made me want to hunt the real thing, wild boar. Do you know he came close to getting a boar once. Skeet shooting doesn't do much except improve your aim, and hurt your shoulder." Here he actually laughed at his own joke.

At least he was talking about guns now, so the captain asked, "Are you a good shot? Was Politis?"

"I am, but Vras was fairly new…"

"How did Politis get involved? He wasn't there to be mesmerized by your father's stories," Geró interrupted.

"No, but our old relatives were boys together, and you know how tight those friendships were."

"But you and Politis were not tight, as you call it."

"How could we be. Most of his family moved to Australia before he was even born. I was told they suffered a lot even before the Germans invaded Greece."

"Did they suffer more than any other Kaminia family? Everyone here knew what was coming. Bands of Loyalists (the underground) were preparing, arming themselves, gathering staples. You are too young to know that."

Fotis cut him off. "I heard that, but what I meant was his mother's uncle was taken away for some reason and sent to work in a foreign country's labor camp. He was never heard from again. She also saw enough killing of Greeks by Greeks in the civil war after Germany. Vras' mother had a breakdown of some kind. She said no child of hers would ever be born here. She threatened to suffocate any newborn baby she had so it would not have to live through the poverty and cruelty that would be left in Greece."

"And you know all this from gossip, right?" Pidalios asked. "Did the entire family leave?"

"What has any of this to do with today? Vras is dead, shot by me." Fotis put both hands over his eyes for a moment. "I'm truly sorry. What I did accidentally is a catastrophe for me. I'll never recover. I just want to go home."

Pidalios handed him a paper napkin and pointed to the red trail of ketchup from the burger on his chin and thought all Fotis was worried about was maybe leaving his thermos up there.

"A few more minutes," the captain said. "Let's continue—about the family."

"If I may continue, captain," Geró intervened. Sakalidis nodded, giving way to his friend. "I seem to recall a similar tragedy in Kaminia's history many years ago, not during hunting, just a murder by gunfire. If I am not mistaken, the shooter was named Grigorakis. Any relation to you, Mr. Grigoris?"

"I'm not sure."

"Not sure? From what I hear he was your grandfather."

He looked up. "Oh, sorry, I'm shook up. He was my grandfather. We shortened the name," Fotis admitted. He acted exhausted and irritated from all the questions. (Stupid questions from stupid cops, he thought.)

"You said your dead friend was married?"

"Yes, how many times are you going…oh, my God, Katina! They have two children. She doesn't know yet, and the kids. I killed her husband, my friend, please…"

"Don't be alarmed," said Pidalios. "The captain sent a very sympathetic, sensitive officer, Toula Vatis. As soon as she got his wife's name and address, she left for Kaminia to inform and comfort them."

"She is our specialist in grief counseling besides being a very good police officer." John added. "Are you married, Fotis?" the captain questioned the man across from him, who had slumped back in his chair as Geró and Pidalios left the room.

"I never really considered it." He reined in the smirk that accompanied the answer. "Never gave it much thought or found the right one."

The captain excused himself and left the room for a moment, closing the door behind him. Re-entering several minutes later, he told Fotis, "My consultants and I have decided you have had enough for today. Yet, I must remind you that new clues or information can come up, so will we be able to count on your being in Kaminia if we need to speak to you?"

"If I'm not at the house in Kaminia, ask around. I am the only master craftsman in the area. Here is my cell phone number." He handed the captain his card. "By the way when can I get my gun back?"

"Not for awhile; it is evidence in a death. It will be checked, and then you will be contacted."

"But I'm not guilty of anything, and I want my property." His voice was demanding.

"In due time," the captain kept his voice level.

"How much time? I want to go hunting."

"When we are finished. The season just started today, and it's two months long."

Sgt, Goovis knocked and opened the door. "Sir, I'm ready to drive Mr. Grigoris home."

Pidalios drove through the village of Katsoulaika and took the narrowing road into Kaminia. All the while Geró sat in the back seat of the shiny silver car. "Watch the ruts. This isn't a well-paved road. Go slower, Pidalios. My spine is getting a jolting back here."

"Neh, neh, [yeah, yeah], Thio." He smiled into the rearview mirror. "Remember, I drove many types of vehicles on unpaved roads in the army. I have it under control. "You, know, Thio, you could stop complaining and look for a small sign with the street name STENO on it. His house is supposed to be at the far end. My eyes fail me on this one."

Geró said, "Could that be the place?" He pointed to a turn, and at the end was an old hamoukela with aged and weathered stone walls. Thick vines seemed to be helping to keep rain off the roof tiles. The place looked abandoned, but Geró spotted a very senior citizen sitting on a rocker under an overhang, built on for shade from the Mediterranean sun.

Pidalios rolled the car to a stop on the gravel near the front. "I'm sure he sees us."

"He is not reacting to the car pulling up," Geró added.

"Possibly he's asleep or dead," joked his nephew.

"What nonsense! Get out of the car and behave yourself. Let me do the talking."

Crushing out the cigarette he had been holding up to the slightly open window, Pidalios got out, let his uncle take the lead but called out, "Excuse us, sir. We are looking for Kyrios Mavrogenis."

"I am Mavrogenis," a surprisingly strong voice accompanied a welcoming wave. "It's nice to have visitors."

After introducing both of them to the all white-haired Mr. Mavrogenis [black beard], Geró said, "Thank you for seeing us. I called ahead, but there was no answer. We are private detectives, consultants to the Sparta Astynomia. Would it inconvenience you to answer a few questions about this village. We are told that you are the man to consult on its history and residents."

"I hope I am able to give you the information you want, but you realize I am a bit older," said the very old man, "and the memory is beginning to fade like a river in a dry spell."

I like this old man, Pidalios thought. Geró was about to continue, but Mavrogenis said, "Young man, please bring two chairs from just inside the door. Then sit and be comfortable, both of you. I prefer speaking at eye level with others. If you're thirsty, I have a bottle of cold, mountain spring water inside on the table. If not, what can I help with?"

Geró told him the circumstances and names involved in the shooting on Tayegatos. The man was already aware of the tragic event. "Village talk spreads quickly."

"We are not here to accuse the man who allegedly shot Vrasithas Politis. Our purpose is to investigate a past event."

"I understand, and I am quite disturbed by today's news. That same young man, Politis, volunteered to finish this sun shade (He pointed up.) after an incompetent, paid workman could not, and he did a wonderful job and refused any payment."

"We have heard about his good character," said Geró. "The story we are looking into may be part of his past family history. It happened many years ago, 1941. The story is that one man shot another here in Kaminia. Can you give us the background on that, or is it another case of Greeks embellishing…"

"…as they are so wont to do," the old man declared." He continued. "In that year a man shot and killed a younger man, named Politis, here in our small central square. His name was Fotis Grigorakis. He was this Grigoris' grandfather, who shot that young man because of a never-proven story that a young girl, Maria—a fifteen year old, had made love with the twenty-something, married, Vrasithas Politis.

"Grigorakis was the self-proclaimed 'protector' of the village. He was a big man, feared by others, and no one ever questioned his judgment. He had picked Maria for an arranged marriage with one of his sons. "I was a witness in this village, and I can verify the truth of this sad story."

"Αλήθεια [al ee thee a-truth]?" broke in a skeptical Pidalios.

He noted a stern look from Geró but not the village historian, who smiled. "It is a bit coincidental and ironic, isn't it. Two shooters: same name, two victims: same name. Maybe it is not always wise to name grandchildren after grandparents, as is traditional here in Greece."

"Excuse my interrupting, sir, please continue."

"Grigorakis shot and killed the younger man because the gossip was that untoward advances were spoken boldly to an unmarried fifteen year old girl from the village. Back then honorable men in remote places all over this country followed a strict behavioral code to protect the virtue of their women. I did say that the dead man was a member of the Politis family, did I not?

"His own wife had given birth to a son, their first child, only a few months before. I must add that the young father previously had been the απολολό πρόβατα [apololo provata-black sheep] of his family—you know, the stray that lost its flock. Then he met the beautiful Aspasia, and she caused his complete turnaround. Then a son, and everything he ever wanted had come true. The whole village was shaken when he was shot for such behavior, if he did it."

"Did what?" asked Pidalios.

"Ah, those days were so different. There were always a few strong-willed, self-appointed heads in some horios. In their own minds they were in the right, policing the actions of all . This particular shooter was always in charge in Kaminia. His pistola was at the ready, and nobody challenged him; they were all afraid. Men like him were bullies, but generally they kept the citizenry on a morally straight path. You know, like law and order in the Old West, neh?" He laughed at his own joke.

Geró spoke. "Throughout history, no matter where, a few with weapons and the use of fear control the many unarmed. My question to you, sir, is did Grigorakis have a secondary motive?"

"Another motive for killing the boy? From my possibly fuzzy memory I understand that the object of this act, Maria Katsouris, was the chosen young woman in a proposed match for the 'sheriff's' son, and now she had been shamed by gossip in her village." He took a sip of water.

Geró cited a Greek philosopher. "Socrates was right. 'Fake words are not only evil in themselves, but they infect the souls with evil.'"

Mavrogenis continued, "So true, because her reputation was now tainted. The word spread, and her purity was also in question. Maybe she had encouraged him? Look what it would do to his wife, κέ τά λοιπα [kay ta leepa-etc.-κτλ]. When a woman's morality was questioned, she was no longer worthy of marriage into a good family, or she was shunned. It seems ridiculous to us in 1995. There were tales of women even being stoned to death. Who was it who said, 'First learn the meaning of what you say, and then speak.'"

"One of our own," replied Geró, "Epictetus."

Pidalios wanted to get back to the history of this village, and he asked, "So, what did happen to Maria? or his wife? the baby?" He hoped for some connection to the present day killing.

"I don't know. Word was that she could no longer stay here, and the supposed marriage she was picked for never came about; she was no good, so they said. She left here, and hearsay had it that she had gone away to Yugoslavia to join the communist movement.

I heard rumors that as she got older, she fought with the underground under the name 'Sorceress.'

"Vrasithas' wife and child left. I think they went to relatives elsewhere, but I can't swear to any of this."

"I'm surprised Maria didn't take the name Vrasithanas, the shadowy reflection on her supposed lover, Vrasithas," Pidalios smirked.

"Now, my friends, I am tired. If I have answered your questions, I'll just sit here on my porch, look out at the mountain and snooze."

"Goodbye, sir. We thank you." Geró and Pidalios shook the man's still strong outstretched hand, and they turned away.

"Wait," Mavrogenis stopped them. "The killer's name was Grigorakis then, but after he was sent to the filthy prison on Γιάρος island, his family used the name Grigoris—maybe from shame?"

"Maybe that's why Fotis conveniently forgot or stumbled over his grandfather's last name at the precinct." said Pidalios.

"I know all this because I was mature at the time and saw or heard it all, said Mavrogenis."

In the car Geró commented on the narrow streets, small traditional homes and lack of modernization. "You know, my nephew, we only got electricity here in our Peloponnesian horios in 1961."

"My father told me that. Not that many years ago, was it?"

"No, but I keep thinking of the past and how it evolved into today—Grigorakis-Grigoris. Killer then-killer now possibly?

Chapter 3

Before he started the car, Pidalios opened his window a few inches for exhaling space. When he wasn't inhaling it, he kept the toxic cigarette close to that opening.

"You are a thoughtful man to go to all that trouble," came the pointed remark from the back seat.

"Thank you, and I am cutting down, if you have been observing."

"Instead of cutting give elimination a try."

Ignoring his concerned uncle, Pidalios asked, "Do you think we should keep looking into the 1941 shooting or just concentrate on the present tragedy?"

"Why not do both. We always get clues from the past. Also, a whitewashed crow won't stay white for long."

"Who said that about a white crow? A cover up, you think?"

"The author of that is an unknown but profound thinker. We will keep investigating past and present until evidence directs us— that is if you agree."

Looking into the rear view mirror at the mostly gray hair behind him, Pidalios nodded his agreement and said, "I follow my leader."

"Now, dear partner, I am getting hungry. Can you step on it?"

"One time it's slow down, then it's step on it," Pidalios quipped as he readied his cell phone when they were outside his uncle's apartment building. Geró got out, thanked his nephew, wished him a good evening and walked the driveway to the building entrance. Pidalios called his aunt, "Buzz him in, Thia."

"Got it," she responded. A moment later her husband entered the open door to their apartment and kissed his wife's proferred cheek. "Well," a smiling Irini said, "any gory details to share over dinner?"

"Something smells like chicken soup— perfect on a chilly November day."

"I took out the cooked vegetables, added the orzo, and it is all ready for you to make into the finest chicken avgolemeno soup in town. The eggs are at room temperature, and the lemons are rolled, halved and pitted. The chicken is deboned and shredded. Go to it at your leisure, my culinary genius."

He did just that after washing up and whipping the eggs into a frenzy, adding broth and lemon juice very slowly. Geró and his wife of many years ate the delicious soup and talked about the latest case. She listened attentively, asking perceptive questions so that she might possibly turn some of this into her latest mystery novel.

Irini, a high school English teacher, had met Geró Peerooney in New York City. After overcoming the 'Greeks married only Greeks' unwritten law, they wed. She moved to Sparta, Greece, with him to his job as a police detective. Later he became a famous private cop for solving the murder of his former corrupt chief. Suffering the ache of only seeing her family sporadically, Irini found her way. Several of her mystery novels were even available now in the very well-stocked Sparta library.

Over dinner the discussion was about the scene in situ and whether a gorge is similar to a ravine. "I think it is called a coulee. Out on the west coast in America, it is a dry gulch, washed away by water," she offered. Finally getting off the synonyms: gorge, abyss, gully and chasm, the description that fascinated Irini was of Kyrios Mavrogenis. "He is a gem! A sense of humor in an old man with such knowledge of history of his village and its environs, sitting alone on a porch in Kaminia. I would enjoy speaking with him, Gerómou. Would he come to dinner, do you think?"

"I think he would be honored by the invitation but decline gracefully. When the case is over, we'll take a ride to his horio; you drive, of course. If he is sitting on his porch, we will bring him a box of glika [glee kah-sweets] and stop for a moment or two."

In the morning Geró was in their sparsely furnished office by 8:30 with his filtro (drip) coffee ready. Pidalios, who drank iced coffee every morning of the year, walked in with one and two small brown bags, containing τηγανόψωμα [tee gan óp soma-fried bread].

He purchased these at a different bakery each day to spread the wealth fairly to businesses in Sparta. Each baker cut off a small hunk of ready bread dough. Instead of baking it in the oven, he fried it. The patron was able to pick cheese on the side or raisins in the dough—a delicious breakfast. While they sipped and chewed, they briefly shared local talk then moved to their itinerary for the day.

They walked to Astynomia headquarters because Geró insisted that consumption of the large piece of fried bread necessitated some exercise. Capt. Sakalidis was the first person they met inside the building. "Good morning, you two. I was just about to get a report from Officer Toula Vatis. She's in my office. Join us?"

The three men greeted Toula and pulled chairs around the captain's metal desk. "Officer Vatis, you met with the widow, Katina Politis, late yesterday. Would you please fill us in?"

Vatis began, "Yes, sir. As soon as she saw me, a uniformed officer, walking to her door, she burst through it and came out yelling, 'My children! Are they hurt?' It took me several minutes to calm those fears, take her inside and get her to sit. I had brought along a bottle of water; I poured some into a glass on the table. The kitchen was very neat and tidy as was the other part of the house that I could see. I then told her that I had some bad news, not about her children but about her husband."

"Did he fall up on the mountain? He went hunting with his friend Fotis. I told him to be very careful up there, not very skilled," she added. "I told her he had been shot and did not survive the shooting, that he was dead."

"Her reaction?" Sakalidis requested.

"Complete hysteria. I immediately put my arm around her and walked her to the couch. I sat next to her and soothed her throughout her sobbing. I had brought ένα σφηνάκι [ena sfee naki-a one shot bottle] of cognac. She did not want it, but I told her it would help — to take small sips.

"Katina told me, 'When I heard the church bells, the dirge for the dead, a little while ago, I never thought it was for Vrasithas. I was wondering which old villager has passed. I thought someone who knew must have called the priest. Oh, my God, how will I go on!' Her grief was extreme. The good thing was that her neighbor, a motherly type and close friend, heard her loud sobbing and rushed through the open door. Kyria [Mrs.] Stathakos, hearing of Katina's loss, took my place, so I could go out to my car and call for a local doctor. Luckily, Kaminia has one on our department list. I called, identified myself, and he came quickly. He gave her some medication to calm her, and he left some sedatives, instructing the neighbor to give Kyria Politis only two per day. My thought was that giving them to the neighbor was questionable.

"He reassured me that there is always a fear of overdose, accidental or otherwise, in such grief-stricken patients. 'Mrs. Stathakos is well-known to me, and she is trustworthy.'

"I have included his name, Dimitri Matritis, MD, in my written report. The friend said she would make sure the priest came, and she would take care of the children for as long as needed. I was assured that she and the Pater [priest] would tell the children as gently as possible the terrible news of their father's death.

"I am now searching for nearby close relatives or other friends to aid her. Should I call any other offices, or do you take care of that, Captain Sakalidis?"

"I will call those departments that should be made aware, and it sounds to me as if you did a thorough and caring job. Thank you, officer."

"One more thing, if I may. I wrote on a card I had with me a quote I learned from Kyrios Peerooney." She glanced at Geró and continued, "It is: 'Death leaves a heartache no one can heal; love leaves a memory no one can steal.' Under it I wrote my name and cell number and that she should call me any time if she needs me. I hope that is all right."

"That quote is from an unknown source, and it was found on a tombstone in Ireland," said Geró, smiling at her. Personally, I think your action was a great kindness, Toula."

Both John and Pidalios nodded their agreement. Officer Vatis left the office. The captain, Geró and Pidalios smiled at her exiting back and stayed for a brief meeting. Pidalios spoke. "With new, thoughtful officers, such as Toula Vatis the Sparta Astynomia is taking a positive turn."

"Thank you. Though something else has been on my mind. I'm troubled a bit. Do you recall, I thought I had seen someone or something on the edge of the other side of the gully? Officer Goovis, Dr. Karis and I all arrived at the same time but in a rush. We looked down on the scene of two men lying face down, one seemingly on top of the other. When we got to them, blood, guns and mayhem—the focus of all, I looked up at the other bank for a split second. At the top I thought I saw either a shepherd, an anxious hunter or maybe it could have been a reflection of light from a shotgun. I just am not sure."

"Since it was an image that made an impression on you, John, it is worth a second look. Did Goovis or the doctor recall seeing anything or anyone?" Geró said.

"I asked them, but both said they had been concentrating on climbing down there to see if any help could be given. Grigoris was in such a state. He was lying face down next to his buddy. When we first saw him, we thought he was wounded or also dead. My full attention was on the scene we faced, but I don't know...maybe I'll go back and look for a local chopanis [shepherd]. Maybe he will know something, or he was looking for a lost sheep. I just can't let it go."

"You have enough on your hands," said Geró. I have a relative up there. He's a shepherd, and they camp near that area where their sheep usually graze. All chopanithes have their own chain of communication. We'll check with him," Geró offered.

"In the next local election here in Sparta, I think you should run for mayor, my friend," the captain replied. "You know everybody, and you would definitely win. For the first time then I would be able to trust my local official completely, but keep that remark confidential." He patted Geró's shoulder as they all left laughing.

In the hall Pidalios said to his uncle, "Maybe a community door to door questioning is in order in Kaminia. A neighbor or cafe owner or customer might know something. It's worth a trip, and there aren't many full time residents in Kaminia. Now that the cold weather is coming many head back to America or Canada. If you have something else to do, I volunteer."

"You are such an industrious partner—never lazy or incompetent. Since driving on bad roads as well as good is such a pleasure for you, maybe you wouldn't mind continuing on afterward to Tripoli to see our friendly lab men, Thodoris and Taki. They might have received slides, blood samples κτλ [etc.] by now and have some report for us. They're your friends, so offer to take them out for a coffee or lunch, on me, of course." He handed his nephew forty drachmas "Enjoy yourselves, and meanwhile I will call Dr. Karis at the hospital. Maybe he set a time for the autopsy. I want to be there."

"Count me out, Thio."

"Count me in," said Sakalidis, coming down the steps from the second floor.

Chapter 4

Before leaving for the Tripoli lab to see the dynamic duo (borrowed from the comics), Pidalios stopped for an iced coffee for the road. He decided to do the door-to-door in Kaminia tomorrow. He called Geró at the office. "Kali mera, Thio, I am leaving for the lab, but I have extra time. I'll pick you up and drop you at Nosokomeio [hospital]…"

…"What's this 'pick you up and drop you stuff?'" Geró snarled. "At that suggestion I'll be a patient there, not an observer at a post mortem. I know you are being helpful and I thank you, but the captain is taking me with him."

Pidalios came back with, "Maybe he'll let you sit in the front seat of the big police car."

"Wise guy, say hello to Thodoris and Taki."

"Θα τα πούμε." [tha ta poume-we'll talk again).

Captain Sakalidis buzzed and joined Geró for a cup of filtro (American) coffee, prepared in the office drip pot. "Some Greeks we are, preferring American style coffee, huh?" commented the captain.

They exchanged small talk and discussed this case. Geró asked John if he had any new recollection to share about the person he thought he saw up on the mountain the day of the shooting.

"Not really, but whoever or whatever I saw was small. Did you get a chance to speak with the chopanis up there?"

"Not yet. Pidalios is at the lab in Tripoli today, and you and I will be at the morgue. I do have it on my list probably for tomorrow." He then related the conversation he and Pidalios had with the old historian Mavrogenis in Kaminia.

"The way history repeats itself is ironic, isn't it, Geró: Over a span of many years two shootings with the same name relatives involved, same village? Maybe we'll get something, and I plan on calling Grigoris in again for more questioning. I'll let you know when. I just don't like his attitude."

The two men were greeted in a tolerant tone by Dr. Karis when they arrived to observe the autopsy. Karis was helping his assistant lay out all the surgical tools needed and told them to put on gowns, hats and gloves. He offered them masks to ward off the scent of death as the draped body of Vrasithas Politis was uncovered under the high powered lamp over the table. Geró refused the mask, and John held a gauze pad in his hand in case the odor was too pervasive. "For years we would put a dab of Vicks under our nostrils," he said.

"Until I took over," said the doctor. "Vicks might block odor, but it can also interfere with findings from smells that are helpful in determining cause. We have extractors that remove most fumes, and I say just get used to it. Generally the odor is not that bad. I once had to perform this surgery on a corpse that was found after a month. Now that was stench!" He turned to his assistant. "Take over Giorgo." The younger man stepped up, made the first Y incision, removed and weighed the organs and brain. Dr.Karis dissected certain parts and spoke his observations aloud in medical terms into a microphone positioned overhead.

Dr. Karis barely spoke to the observers, and, when he did, it was almost inaudible to them. Frustrated by that and the lack of communication, Geró and John interrupted with a question or two so they could gain a bit of information and pretend they were there for a reason. The doctor would have none of it. After the organs had been placed into the body's cavity, and it was sewn up, he turned to Capt. Sakalidis and the detective and led them into the hall.

Geró looked a little pale but reassured the doctor that he was just fine. He did ask, "Can you tell us anything right off? It was extremely difficult to hear in there." His voice had an edge to it.

"The damage showed that the victim was shot in the back with a shotgun. After I examine the slug I removed and the tissue, I will forward my findings to you both. You said he was shot at close range; therefore, I am interested in finding out just how close and what was the secondary tissue damage. Other than that, what we have here is a fairly young man who was in good health—no cancer or heart problems. Probably he would have lived a good, long life. I'll walk you out; I need a cigarette." He rushed ahead of them after this very skimpy report.

"Now that we have had little cooperation, we seem to be on our own," said John to Geró.

"My question will concentrate on the angle of entry. I am glad Pidalios wasn't here. I discourage his heavy smoking every chance I get. If he saw the doctor run out for a smoke, he would have been even more armed with comebacks for my criticisms."

John frowned as he said, "Other than lots of blood and guts we didn't get anything to help with evidence, did we?" He was disappointed and walked with his friend to the car. On the way back to Sparta, they listed the steps in what Geró always called 'what now?' and discussed who might offer clues in this case.

As Irini got older, her arthritis gave her severe knee pains. She probably could have searched the medical registry in Athens for a specialist, but once a year she used the barking pain as her excuse for a trip home alone to Long Island, New York, for appointments with her rheumatologist, Dr. Manuela Marinescu, not only a great doctor, but also a compassionate woman, whom Irini now thought of as a friend. Dr. Marinescu had been born in Romania. Irini lived in a Mediterranean culture in Greece, so the two women shared life experiences in the way of life in each country.

Irini also used the need for knee injections as a time to visit remaining family and friends. Geró was usually unable to accompany her because of his work. He understood that the Hyalgan (gel injections), made from rooster combs, staved off pain, her growing crankiness and allowed her a guilt free vacation from him and Sparta. Both of them were of the belief that people in a solid marriage still needed a break from each other *once in a while. The happiness of reunion only made a marriage stronger.*

Irini had two appointments scheduled with Manuela, and she arrived a few days before to the reality that the doctor was in another branch office on the two booked Wednesdays. It didn't make much difference except for the few extra miles to drive. She rented a Mini Cooper, her favorite car, and drove to Smithtown for the first appointment at an unfamiliar location.

Searching for a building number, she passed the driveway, not easily spotted among tightly packed buildings on doctor row. She parked in the next building's lot on more elevated ground with a grassy embankment down to her intended destination. Irini left the car and decided she could walk on the grass, not realizing it was slippery from the morning's sprinkler bath. She stepped in her Tom's rubber soles. The next thing she remembered was hitting her forehead on the concrete below after an ass-over-head tumble. It really hurt, and she felt blood running down her face and saw it dripping into her open purse, where she was feeling for tissues to staunch the flow. She hoped no one had witnessed her embarrassment as she lay there attempting to gather herself together and get up.

Elevated adrenaline helped in reaching the doctor's office door. As Irini entered, she was aware of gasps and 'OMGs' as several staff ran to her, put her in a chair inside and applied compresses to her head. Soothing tones were interrupted by her friend, Dr. Marinescu, who rushed to her and immediately ordered a call for an ambulance.

Irini tried to argue with the police and the ambulance EMT, but no one paid attention as she was ushered into the vehicle with flashing lights. Hearing very high blood pressure read aloud into a phone, her age and a description of her wounds and the words 'possible concussion or skull fracture,' she remained quiet. After six hours of CT scans, MRIs, stitches, tests and bandaging, etc., the was released into her American relatives' custody. She was told to have the stitches in her forehead removed in a week. Allowing for the seven hours difference, she called Geró. He said he would come. She told him she just needed quiet, rest and those damned knee shots in the next two weeks.

Irini with a black eye, a yellow, green and purple spotted face, which took a month to clear, finally went home to Greece, where her concerned husband and nephew met her at Eleftherios Venizelos airport in Athens.

After welcoming gentle hugs and checks to make sure she was all right, Geró chided her, "What a story you conjured up to get an extended vacation from us."

Pidalios added and equally snarky remark. "Why didn't you just say you were tired of Thio?"

Irini knew she was safe at home, but she said, "What? No flowers?" It made the three laugh because they knew she hated ceremony and displays.

In the car the near tragic incident brought to mind a similar one during the time when she and Geró were visiting in New York. It was the last time he ever drove a car.

She needed to stop at an ATM, and, since he was driving, he pulled up at their closed bank. He waited in the still running car as she got out to use her debit card. She put her card into the slot that opened the booth for customers. No matter how many attempts she made, the green light did not come on to allow access.

She spoke to her husband through her open passenger door. "It just won't work." A rushed, impatient Geró kept shouting instructions to her as she stood there. She turned, walking back, and said angrily, "Never mind; just forget it." She was about to get back into the car.

Geró jumped out saying, "I'll do it." He forgot that the running car was still in reverse gear. It rolled back, the door knocking Irini down flat on her back. Her head hit the pavement hard, and she could not get up. Her hand was torn up, and a growing bump was quickly rising on the back left side of her head. She was lying on the street crying.

He had jumped back into the driver's seat and stopped the moving car. By the time he got to her, he had vowed that he would never drive again. She recovered, and Geró kept that promise. Pidalios had driven him ever since.

Chapter 5

"Thio? I"m leaving Tripoli soon. I saw Thodoris and Taki and gave them your regards. They said, 'Who's he?'"

"You are slipping, my nephew. You can do better than that. Just tell me you forgot to say hello to them, and I'll forgive you. You also forgot to take them to lunch on my dime, right?"

"If truth be told, they asked for you as soon as I walked into the lab. They didn't have time for lunch, but they thanked you for the gesture."

"Backed up with work?"

"Thodoris is so slim, probably from skipped lunches. Taki is going bald early—stress not starvation. I walked to Klimatakia [the grapevine] and had a platter of mezethakia [appetizers] delivered from you, okay?"

"Sometimes you are a real sport; you should have put your name on it too, but thank you."

"Now I'm hungry. I'll be there about six. Check with Thia, and I'll swing by and take you two to Parori for their famous chicken."

"I think she'll be pleased, but this time it will be my treat."

"Great. See you then, and the dynamic duo said they will get the results to us as fast as possible."

The culinary delights in the restaurant that evening brought remembrances of thirty years with Geró Peerooney, the husband whose Greek name means 'strong fork.' It was such a fitting name for a man of many appetites—not just his voracious consumption of Greek food.

Since they first married, he noticed her eyes growing wider at the size of his portions, taken from the bowls and platters she put on the table. He would cite one of his many favorable quotes about food, such as, "'What I say is that, if a man really likes potatoes, he must be a pretty decent sort of fellow,' A. A. Milne."

Irini, not to be outdone, countered with, "I am a better person when I have less on my plate.' Elizabeth Gilbert-'Eat, Pray, Love.'"

Now that they were older, she put out smaller amounts, much more salad and vegetables. The magnificent crusty Greek bread was now served in a smaller basket she had found in a local variety store. The sides and bottom were padded with napkins so the basket looked fuller. Most importantly, she never failed to give him credit for beginning and sticking to a walking program: four kilometers each morning, where he passed several bakeries without stopping in for a koulouri. As a result he maintained his healthy weight.

Dinner in Parori was a delight, not only because of the food, but also from the pleasure of each other's company.

Pidalios quipped, "Thia, bread?" as he offered the basket. "Oops, I forgot you probably already had your one hunk of the month."

"Don't get me wrong," she said. "I could eat the entire basket of bread, slathered with butter or oil, but I still remember how we came to Greece for two months after we first married. I credit the bread as well as the food and fabulous desserts with my thirty pound weight gain. I can still see my father, blowing up his cheeks when he first saw me again."

Pidalios laughed and said, "but he was just kidding, right?"

"No, he wasn't," answered Geró. "She was so miserable she quit smoking and joined Weight Watchers on the same day." Geró began to laugh.

"I was very unhappy. After several attempts in groups that were not inclusive, or maybe it was just my fault—not mentally ready, I stopped. Losing weight plus giving up smoking at the same time was an uphill battle. Luckily, your Thio supported me in my several failed attempts." Geró smiled angelically. "Then I heard about a welcoming leader, Fran Posner, who succeeded because of her personality, her approach and methods the others had not used. It worked, and once I became a free lifetime member because of my weight loss, I quietly nicknamed her 'Perfect Posner.' The woman was kind, always smiling and prepared to offer her time and advice one could follow, only if asked for. I never did quit

WW. I always drop in on a Fran Posner meeting whenever I am back in New York."

The three went on to stories of Pidalios' always tall, slim frame, no matter what he ate. He denied ever eating too much unless, of course, it was forced on him. He loved makaronatha as much as his uncle, and he ate it by the platter full, infused with olive oil and heaps of grated cheese. "What's your line, Thio? 'Humor keeps us alive. Humor and food. Don't forget food. You can go a week without laughing.'"

"Not my line, someone named Joss Whedon."

When fresh fruit arrived for dessert, Irini told the story of the old days—when Geró still drove a car. They used Pidalios' brother Dimitri's car, a big old Accord, that he had left behind when he relocated to Australia after he married Mary.

One day Geró pulled the stick shift car nose-in to the fence in the parking lot at Katounas Bakery out on Gytheio Rd. They were buying sweets as a gift for a dinner host, and always a box to take home. When they came out of the store, Geró started the car but had difficulty shifting into reverse. The car kept going forward. He would clamp down on the brake and try again and again.

Irini feared they would crash through the fence into the yard next door. Geró was extremely agitated, and noticed a police car, pulling into the lot and parking next to them. Two young officers got out and entered the bakery.

"Geró, you are losing patience. Ask one of them to shift this monster."

"I will not. I can do this! It's just an old car, not used often, probably rusty." He kept trying the noisy shift, and the car kept inching forward. In the mirror he saw the officers coming out; he got out and quietly requested their help. One of them got into the driver's seat, put it into reverse, backed it out a ways and showed Geró how to move the gear shift in this car. Irini returned his smile, and her husband thanked him. When the police drove away, Geró, now back in control, snapped, "I could have done that, but you were in a rush."

"Don't blame me for a red-faced moment; let me add to that. They recognized you as the famous private dick. I'm surprised they didn't ask for your autograph."

Chapter 6

Geró reached for the phone and answered, "Λέγατε?" [leg ah tay-speak]. He listened. "Good morning, John. Just fine, and you? Yes, she's fine too. In fact, we went to Parori last night with Pidalios—terrific chicken, yes. If you and your wife would care to join us next time…"

"…Thanks, my friend. She likes sitting up there, looking down on the lights of Sparta at night, almost as much as she likes the food. Listen, I'm calling for two reasons. Did Pidalios get any results from the lab yesterday?"

"Not yet, but they're putting a rush on it. Maybe we'll get something later today; I'll call you."

"I'd appreciate it. Also, I'd like the two of you to be here later. Grigoris is coming in."

"What time? Did you ask him to come in?"

"Everything is turning sour in this case. I very politely requested that he come in at nine this morning, but he told me he would be busy. I said when would be convenient. He asked if this was really necessary, and gave me the excuse that he was still in shock over his part in Politis' killing. I said that we only want to talk to him—to straighten out some confusion."

"And?"

"He finally agreed to be here at four, but he said he couldn't stop in for long. I don't trust this guy somehow, especially because he finished by asking if he could get his gun back."

"I'll tell Pidalios; he's not here yet, but we will be there, and don't let this guy get to you. John. He seems to be a complex character and a bit contrary to boot. I'll be there to witness and watch."

"Thanks."

Pidalios and Geró walked into the police precinct a bit earlier than four. John apologized and told them Grigoris still wasn't there. "You know Greeks, always late," joked Pidalios.

They waited in the captain's office after refusing coffee. Finally, an unhurried, unapologetic Fotis Grigoris was announced at 4:25. "I put him in room alpha," said a police officer. The cops had a private joke. Room alpha was for questioning; room omega was for the doomed.

At 4:35 the captain, Geró and Pidalios walked in, said hello and thanked Grigoris for coming in.

"A little impatient, aren't you?" asked the captain. "I heard you asking an officer where we were. The police have more than this case, you know."

"I don't have much time" was his response.

"Then let's get right to it. We have some concerns over details in this case," said the captain.

"Okay."

"Our consultants visited a gentleman, a learned man, who lives in your village. He seemed to know a great deal about Kaminia's history."

"He's supposed to be smart, but remember, he's a very old man," said Fotis, obviously knowing Mavrogenis.

"We found him knowledgeable and quite perspicacious," Geró added.

"If you say so."

"I do," Geró responded, thinking Fotis didn't know what perspicacious meant.

"Why am I here?"

"Kyrios Mavrogenis told us that years ago,1941 to be exact, a villager named Fotis Grigorakis, your grandfather, shot and killed a young man, named Vrasithas Politis. Ironic, isn't it?" Geró baited Fotis.

"As I said before, when we were in here that sad day, you told the same tale. To all of you I say, asked and answered."

"It's not a tale," spit out the captain. "Answer again. Humor us."

"I guess it's oddly similar. According to my father it did happen, but you're talking about the pre-war 40s, about the honorable men in very small horios like Kaminia. They were proud men, the protectors. They would not tolerate certain actions, one of those was dishonoring women, you know, ruining their reputations. The brave men took care of the bad guys."

Geró finished that narrative. "So, your grandfather pulled his pistola and murdered a young man. Is that why you switched your last name to Grigoris?"

"You guys watch too many 'Zorba the Greek' movies," snarled Grigoris.

"There was only one," Pidalios corrected him.

"My grandfather was the victim of village gossips. Why, I even heard old wives' tales about a father who killed his own daughter because old biddies spread the word that she had sex with some guy."

"Did your grandfather have a lawful motive? The reason we bring up this 'old wives' tale, as you call it, is that you too claim to have killed, accidentally, of course," said Sakalidis.

"It WAS an accident. Why would I kill my friend? I can't help it that I tripped, and my gun went off. Do I need a lawyer?"

"No, not yet. We are just curious about history repeating itself—although stranger things have happened."

"We looked into the 1941 death," said Geró. "We want to fill you in. Feel free to offer additions or opinions."

"You don't have to waste my time with your details. I never met my grandfather.He was wrongfully dishonored when the cop from nearby..."

"...That was an officer located in Xerokambe at the time. Your relative was arrested on a charge of murder, not on some local's whim."

"My father told me it outraged the men of Kaminia, who thought his father did the right thing, and, if life had not been so bad in those years, they would have rioted and freed him. He was a hero to them, a man of honor."

"We are not here to discuss the men who were considered protectors then," said the captain. We do know he was immediately taken in front of a district magistrate and just as swiftly found guilty. A poor man was Fotis Grigorakis. He had no money for legal battles.

He was sent to an infamous prison on the island of Γιάρος [Giaros]."

"My family said it was horrible there," said Grigoris.

"Geró continued, "Conditions there, as in other Balkan prisons of the time were hellish at best. With all the political turmoil and fears over Germany, preparing to invade Greece, the man was forgotten, even by his staunchest supporters and community friends, and he faded in the memories of his relatives who were far away. Your grandmother was left to take care of her surviving son, your father."

"So, you think the injustice my grandfather suffered caused me to shoot Vras? Are you crazy? It's 1995, man, and I never even met my παππου (pappou-grandfather)."

"Neither did Vrasithas Politis get a chance to meet his grandfather, whose wife Aspasia was left with a two month old son, plus she suffered the lingering doubts of her dead husband's fidelity as well as poverty. She got out and moved with his son to live with family in Australia. One of the people we talked to said she remembers Aspasia saying she would rather smother her son than allow him to grow up in that horio."

"It was a tragedy for all. We talked to other people in Kaminia besides Mavrogenis," Pidalios continued. One of the senior residents remembers your grandmother, abandoned, with family to feed and no money; she did her best. Her garden yielded vegetables, and she still had a few chickens. The occasional bit of money and clothing from the local priest was helpful but meager. The woman, who lived near her, said she became more depressed. Finally, after several years she got word that her other son Yianni was dead in the war; she too died very soon after."

"I know that. I heard that story," said Fotis, "but I don't even know how she died—why? because my grandfather wasn't there?"

"From poison," Geró stepped in. "Rumor had it that she boiled oleander leaves and poisonous mushrooms into a strong tea, which she drank. The villagers and the priest saw to her burial and your father basically made out on his own.

"Your grandfather and the surviving inmates, forgotten by the broken system after the war, were kept captive longer than their sentences. When he finally got out, he was a sick man. He died before he could find your father."

"So, what's your point? My father managed, grew up, got work, married my mother, and he is a fine man, and the horror story ends."

"Not quite," said Sakalidis. "Was there a third friend on the hunt?"

"No, why, did you find one?"

"No."

"Did Vrasithas know your grandfather killed his?"

"No, at least I am unaware if he did. We never talked about it, and why are you asking about a third person?"

"What happened to his mother, his father?"

"Whose? Vras'?"

"Any of the above."

"Excuse me," he said sarcastically, "If I never even met my grandparents, how the hell would I know about his? Can I go now?"

"Do you use Fisherman's Friend cough drops?"

"What?"

"You heard me."

"Can't say I've ever sucked on them." Fotis smirked.

"Why did you take Politis hunting with you?"

"Because I felt like it! What is this? Do you guys think I kidnapped and killed my friend, or do you have anything to charge me with?"

"We are waiting for test results, but we'll let you know. For now you are free to go," said Capt. Sakalidis.

Without another word or smirk Grigoris got up and stormed out. The three men sat stunned. "This malaka really troubles me," said John. "His family history is filled with terrible events. Even though he doesn't seem affected by it, somehow I wonder why he never cared about looking back, finding out anything."

Geró said, "Maybe he already knows, is bitter and pretends he doesn't care. Every Greek I know can give a precise rundown of family trees, names of not only first cousins, but also second cousins, grand and great grandparents, where they themselves fit and where each one lives or lived."

"It's a fact," added Pidalios. "My Thia Irini has always commented on the astonishing family knowledge of every Greek she meets. She claims we are all obsessed. Thio tells her that some unknown writer said, 'Some family trees have beautiful leaves, and some have just a bunch of nuts. Remember, it is the nuts that make the tree worth shaking.'" He laughed.

"And you are one of those," Geró said. "Tomorrow we will go up on the mountain and talk to my second cousin on my father's side, the chopanis. I want to see if he knows anything about your ghost, John. Do you want to come along?"

"Yes, I want to clear that up, if possible."

Chapter 7

They had decided to let Pidalios drive. He knew where to find his uncle's cousin up on Tayegatos. Geró was in his usual seat behind the driver, and John took the passenger seat. It was a cool November morning, but the sun was shining. "Maybe such a sunny day is a good omen," Pidalios said.

"At least for the sheep," John put on his sunglasses.

"If we find my cousin Mitros, you will see that he is a bit standoffish because he doesn't know you. His main job is as the voskos [attendant] of his flock. I will tell him that you are a policeman and my friend, so he will be more forthcoming."

Pidalios made some tricky moves with the car on the narrow road, and Geró called out, "There he is. Park wherever you can."

They got out and stopped at the edge of the road to take a moment to appreciate the magnificent view of Greece and all its glory from up there.

"Too bad you didn't bring your γελίτσα [gelitsa-hand carved cane], Thio. All the old guys use them up here."

John's hand and fake cough covered his amusement. Geró ignored Pidalios' remark and said, "Look for his shepherd's crook (staff). Did you know it is also a defensive weapon: 'thy rod and thy staff' from the Bible. I've read that is the origin of 'Spare the rod and spoil the child.'" He glanced at his nephew. The three climbed down to the chopanis, who acknowledged them with that weapon, waved as they approached.

Introductions over, they exchanged family names and news. After the chopanis said, "Sakalidis? Are your parents from Mystra by any chance. My grandmother's cousin was a Sakalidis and lived there, so close to Sparta."

"I heard the same thing from a friend, but I don't think so, a different family perhaps." John went on to explain the death nearby on November 1 and how he had just a glimpse of what he thought was a person, located up above the death scene. "Is it possible that you or one of the other herdsmen in the area had seen or would know anything, even a minor detail—you know something unusual from that morning? Witness information often helps us."

"Maybe it was another hunter? a lost sheep? Was this early or late morning?" The shepherd didn't know anything. He had not been at the place the captain described but promised to ask other chopanithes. Mitros offered them some of the next batch of fresh feta his wife prepared.

"Could be I was just seeing things," a disappointed captain said as they drove away, not knowing Mitros would get in touch just a few days later.

Pidalios' cell phone played the opening bars of his latest favorite song. He put it on speaker, and the voice of Thodoris greeted them and gave the lab report thus far: "The clump of long dark hair is human, not animal, and it is from a woman. I know that because of the hair product and the scent. Also, the footprint cast, that you said was facing down into the crime area, is very small. Possibly it is from a young boy or more probably from a woman of small stature. It is European size 36-37 or a 6 American. It could even have been a boy wearing a female's shoes."

For once Pidalios made no remarks but simply noted what Thodoris told them. Sakalidis asked if the red bow, perfectly tied on the bush, showed any evidence.

"No, captain, except it had a smudge, dark in color, and we are still working on that as well as checking for possible prints and saliva traces on the foil and cough drop box. I'm sorry for the delay, but we do not want to make a careless report to you."

From the back seat Geró said, "Your work is appreciated once again, Thodoris. Thank Taki as well."

Pidalios looked at the captain for further questions and ended the call, telling Thodoris he'd see them soon. "Well, now I'm interested—a small woman's shoes and hair. It sounds as if you were right, captain."

"If Mitros doesn't get in touch in a week, maybe we'll go back up and claim that feta his γινεκα [yee-nec-ah-wife] makes. I'm hungry.

John, Pidalios, let's have lunch at Maniatis Hotel—my treat."

Lunch was a selection of tasty dishes they shared: horiatiki salata [village salad], wonderful warm bread and sides of spanakorizo [spinach and rice] and keftethes [tiny meatballs in avgolemeno sauce]. Conversation was limited because the dining room was packed, and the low ceilings elevated the volume of voices to unbearable noise levels. Then they dropped John at the precinct with the promise to stay in touch if any of them found out something.

A few days later Geró was accompanying Irini through the maze of stalls and tables in the outdoor Sparta farmers' market, which was an anticipated Wednesday and Saturday event. Growers, small and large brought their choice produce into town at dawn and jockeyed for the best spaces to set up tables to display their wares. A common sight was shoppers, carrying heavily laden bags as they shopped for fresh fruits, vegetables and even clothing, piled on tables on the fringes of the several street market. Some growers had learned sales could be improved over just calling out to customers. They might offer free tidbits on toothpicks or a swirl of their honey on a piece of cracker. Cut up red, juicy tomatoes were displayed on a plate, or tiny mesh bags of dried herbs were in a basket on the table. Scent filled the air.

Irini always went to the market because she could select fresh greens to stew or some juicy red tomatoes, which were unblemished. There was always a possibility of running into a friend or relative. Today Geró pretended to come along only to help carry bags. He always managed to select some melon or unusual vegetable he 'hadn't had since his mother used to cook it.'

As they turned the corner to Λυκούργου (Lee cour goo), they saw his cousin. "Yasou, Mitros," said Irini. It's so nice to see you. Did I thank you for the wonderful tub of yogurt. Your son brought it—handsome young man. And your wife, she's fine?"

"Neh, neh, my son brought your thanks and the shawl back to her. She loved the warmth of it, good for cold nights up there."

"I'm glad."

"Geró, I was coming to see you after I sold all my yogurt. Can we sit and talk a few minutes? I may have information."

Irini spoke up. "I must get home to prepare these greens. We bought too many. You two have your talk," and, saying goodbye, she turned to walk the three blocks home.

Geró led Mitros to a corner kafenion for coffee, and once they were served, the waitress moved on. Geró placed drachmas on the bill she left.

"I asked my friends up there if they saw or spoke to anyone else that day. You did say the captain thought it was a small person."

"That's what he thought, but he could be wrong."

"He was right," said Mitros. "Another chopanis was looking for a wanderer from his flock. As he walked the rim of the hill, you know, maybe it fell over. He looked ahead and spotted a woman, dressed all in black, walking away from the place you mentioned. There are small bushes and an outcrop there."

"Did he speak to her. Was he sure it was a woman?"

"No, he waved and called out to her, but she did not answer. She looked at him but put on large glasses and Ξεφανιςτηκε [ksef-an-ees-tee-keh—disappeared]."

"Could he identify her if he saw her?"

"I didn't ask."

'Well, at least we now know it was definitely a woman the captain saw. Did he notice anything she was carrying away—a bundle or extra clothes or...I don't know."

"He wasn't sure, but he said maybe a bag of some kind. I wish I could help you more."

"Don't worry. What you found out was more than we could have hoped for. If it's necessary, would that man talk to us? What is his name?"

"Tsengos, family from Sotira."

"Ah, Sotira," Geró visibly beamed at the remembrance from his youth. His family stayed up there every year as part of the 'escape the heat' summer community from Anogia. "My mother and grandmother grew the best tasting vegetables in their garden in that soil, and the mountain spring ran cold. I never sleep as restfully as I did in that sod house or outside under the stars.

"Forgive me, I digress. I want to thank you, Mitros, not only have you given us a possible lead but also you brought me a wonderful memory. If you see Tsengos, thank him for me, and we will be in touch. So good to see you, regards to your wife."

He got up and walked directly to Astynomia headquarters to see the captain. It was many streets from here, but the walk would do him good. Entering the precinct he saw Sgt. Goovis and asked if Capt. Sakalidis was there.

"Over here, Geró," John heard him and signaled to him. "I've seen you more in the past few days—something new happen?" he said when he saw his friend's expression.

"Our first possible break, John, and it came from you. I just met with my cousin Mitros. He brought the name of a witness to what you saw that morning. I can only praise you on your observation skills." He gave Sakalidis the details learned from the chopanis.

"Can we meet with this man Tsengos?"

"He said he would cooperate."

"But we have no photo shots for him to identify. Maybe she was just a hunter, but then why wouldn't she stop when he called out to her. Where do we go from here?"

"It's a start. We have a bit of a description of her. Plus it may be her hair we found. From little bites the feast grows, John. Check your sources, and Pidalios and I will get to work. We'll get back to you about this man Tsengos." He shook the captain's hand and left for home.

Chapter 8

"Captain Sakalidis, please. This is Geró Peerooney."

"Sorry, sir. The captain is on his way to Athens for a meeting at headquarters. He won't be back until Friday. Can I take a message? Do you want him to call you?"

"No, just tell him I….Never mind, I'll call him after he returns. It's not important."

Geró and Pidalios were going back up Tayegatos to speak to the shepherd Tsengos. He had seen the woman, and maybe they could squeeze more information from him.

They met Mitros where he said his sheep would be grazing, and he had the man with him. "My friends, this is Tsengos. I'm glad you got here now because he has to get back. His young son is with the flock."

Tsengos shook hands with them and said, "and he is a novice, only eleven, but he is trying his best to learn."

"As long as he's willing," Pidalios said.

"Tsengos," said Geró, "a great nickname. I remember my grandmother referring to her friend's husband as 'Tsengos.'"

"I've always been called that. After all, it does mean herder, shepherd, so it fits me, right?" He laughed loudly through discolored, nicotine-stained teeth. "Mitros tells me you want to know about the woman I saw."

"Would you mind telling us everything you remember about her? If we have any questions, we'll stop you," said Pidalios.

"That day I was looking for one of my young ones that wandered away. I worried maybe it had fallen over into the bottom, so I walked the rim, watching for it in all directions. I heard a noise that sounded like shotguns, but it was so windy, dark and there were things blowing everywhere, and I thought it had to be the hunters or else rock slides. I was watching out for my own skin too. Some of them are crazy, shooting boom, boom." He gestured as if he held a shotgun.

"Wait, you're saying you heard sounds like shotguns—more than one?"

"That's right."

"Were the sounds close together, far apart…."

"One on top of the other. That's why I was watching out for my own ass plus looking for my stray," he answered Geró.

"Did you see a shooter or anyone with a gun?"

"The only person I saw was that small woman I told Mitros about. There are bushes and a rocky outcrop there. She stepped out; I called out to her."

Pidalios asked, "And she was dressed all in black, you said?"

"Black, dark brown—a cape, I call it."

"Like a poncho?"

"I think—heavy wool, goes over the head, neh? She had just put it on and was surprised when she saw me. She quickly put on her sunglasses, flipped her hood up, grabbed her bag and took off."

"How far away from her were you?"

"Ten meters or so."

"Do you have good vision?"

"I think I do."

Geró said, "Tsengos, I know we are keeping you, but did you see the men down at the bottom of the hill?"

"No, I was so surprised by the woman, that I didn't look around or down. I was too busy calling out to her. I wanted to ask if she had seen my little sheep. I just thought she was rude. I dunno, maybe she thought I would hurt her?"

"No, we don't think that was the reason. There was a dead man below, and his friend who might have shot him, right down from where she stood. Maybe she saw something and got scared. Was she carrying anything?"

"I think it was a big dark σακούλα [sac koola-bag, purse]."

"You didn't catch up to her?"

"No, I couldn't have, and I was worried about finding my sheep."

"On more question. Had you ever seen her before?"

"I'm a shepherd. I rarely get into town."

They thanked him and apologized for taking his time and told him that when his son became the big voskos, he'd get a chance to relax before the winter fire. They left so he could get back to work.

In the car talk was about their new information. "That was certainly worth the time," said Pidalios. "He was such a willing talker that I almost wanted to offer some drachmas to him."

"Good thing you didn't; he would have been insulted, but, cigarette lover, did you notice his teeth?"

"I did. Never mind that. He told us what she was wearing and exactly where she was. I think we should go back to Kaminia and ask around. Who is she, and why would she have been up there if she was not a hunter? Maybe she witnessed the shooting and that's why she ran."

"You're right, and the lab agrees that the long black hair, caught on the bush, was a woman's because of scent and product."

"We're just getting started. Let's talk again with Mavrogenis."

"Head for Kaminia right now. Can you call your Thia and put me on." Pidalios pulled over and called. After saying hello to Irini, he handed the phone to his uncle. "Irinimou, yes, we talked to Tsengos. He cleared a few things up, but now we're on our way to Kaminia to see if Kyrios Mavrogenis is at home."

"Stop at Katounas bakery and get him a box of glika from me."

"Not this time. I'll wait until you and I are going. It should come from you. Is there anything for supper, or should I go to the market on my way home."

"When did you ever go to a food store, you faker. You just want to know if I cooked. I just made arni (lamb) and hilopites (noodles). It fits, you know, sheep? shepherd?"

"Very apt. I'll tell Mavrogenis that my wife wants to meet him and bring him treats. I think I'm jealous," he chuckled.

"Don't be. I merely want to speak with another intelligent man to get historical data for my next book. Remember all the research I had to do for 'Valtaki Cove?"

"I do, and I still must make up for that missed dinner there last week. I look forward to your dinner later."

"You were laughing, Thia making jokes again?"

"Yes, and I always humor her, pardon the pun. Now drive."

In Kaminia they spotted Kyrios Mavrogenis walking toward his house. Pidalios stopped the car and offered him the front passenger seat for a ride home.

"Thank you. I was just out for my walkabout, and I had to get my loaf of bread, fresh and still warm. He turned to look at Geró in the back seat and asked after his health.

"I'm fine. I always sit back here. It gives me a space of my own, and I escape my nephew's smoking."

Pidalios just glared at him in the mirror. When they arrived at Mavrogenis' house, he asked if the gentleman had a few moments to talk to them.

"Definitely, but I prefer talking on my porch."

Once they were all settled there, Geró asked if he could tell them anything more on the subject of the Grigoris-Politis shooting. "We were just up there again and spoke to two local shepherds. One actually saw a petite, dark haired woman on the day of the shooting."

"He saw her at the scene of the crime?" asked Mavrogenis.

"Not down at the actual scene-but up above. Could you tell us about the woman Maria Katsouris, the woman who was shunned in 1941? I have no facts. I was wondering where she went, who she was, or what really happened to her. There may be no connection."

"I see. Well, she was from this horio as was the whole cast of characters in that tragedy. I told you she was the young woman, chosen in a match to marry the 'sheriff's son; however, once she was caught (and I use that word very loosely), her life was over here. No one would speak to her."

"Was it only an accusation, or it came to fruition?" asked Geró.

"Not that I ever heard. Her life and those of all the others in the families were ruined. She left the village. I do not know how or who helped her. The rumor was that she went to

Eastern Europe, but how? a young girl like that! I think the truer version is that she went to Athens, joined and fought in the resistance and became a communist. They were all banned from Greece until the 1990s. Actually, this is all hearsay; you will have to get in touch with government sources to find out what happened to her. The problem is there may be no records. She was fifteen at the time; she would be in her early seventies, I think. There is an abandoned house, a hovel actually, her family had, but it has been empty for so many years. If you follow this road about pentakosa metra (half a kilometer), you can see it-abandoned."

"Once again, thank you. I told my wife Irini, former teacher who now writes mystery novels, about our last visit, and she wants to meet you. She said she could gain historical notes and other knowledge about our country."

"Tell her any time you are in Kaminia, she would be welcome. I'd enjoy hearing about her books."

"She will share them with you, and thank you, sir," said Pidalios. "I've read them, and they are enjoyable." He put the chairs back in the house, and they followed directions to the old Katsouris house. Mavrogenis was right. It was run down. They got out of the car, walked up through all the wild growth and knocked. No one answered, so they felt free to look through a dirty, broken shutter into the big room. There appeared to be signs of someone having been there. A rolled up mat and ragged quilt were next to the fireplace. Maybe gypsies or travelers looking for shelter had been there. The room was filthy except the one area that had been carelessly swept to clear space.

Chapter 9

"Kyria Politis?" Pidalios knocked lightly on the widow's door. When there was no answer but he heard movement inside, he gently rapped once more and called out her name again. The door opened, and a woman looked out. "Are you Kyria Politis?"

"Neh, Who are you?"

My name is Pidalios. This is my partner Γερό Πυρούνι [Geró Peerooney]. We are consultants to the Sparta Astynomia. Are you up to a few questions? We are looking into your husband's death."

Eyes, still red from too many tears, looked at him. "I spoke to Officer Vatis already, so why are you here?"

Geró spoke up. "Kyria, we tried to call first, but there was no answer. I hope you do not fear our appearance here. Maybe you would prefer to call the Astynomia to check our identity before talking to us."

"It is all right; I have heard of you before. Please come in." She held the door open wider.

"Thank you. We won't take much time."

"Do you mind sitting with me in the kitchen. My children are playing outside, and I want to watch them. May I offer coffee?"

"Thank you, no," Pidalios answered. "We know you have been through a terrible loss, and we are checking all loose ends, so we can help the police close this, and you can be left in peace."

She brought her tissue from her pocket to dab an escaping tear and nodded her readiness. Geró asked, "Was your husband an enthusiastic hunter?"

"No, actually this was his first time. Oh, he was a good shooter. Fotis had taught him all about the shotgun and taken him out to shoot, practice, I mean."

"Did Vrasithas enjoy the hunt?" As soon as he said it, he knew it was thoughtless. "I'm sorry," he said softly.

"I never found out if he did," and she cried harder.

Pidalios tried to console her by telling her how Mavrogenis had said Kyrios Politis was a fine young man—willing to help anyone in the village.

"He was the best," she smiled as she spoke through trembling lips.

"Fotis was his friend? or just someone to hunt with?" Pidalios had to examine that relationship.

"I'm not sure. He did not socialize that much with Fotis. Mainly the friendship centered around guns, hunting. I think Fotis needed a hunting buddy. I just wish my husband had not been that man."

"It sounds as though you did not like Fotis."

"It's not a question of like or dislike. We had nothing in common, and he does not have a wife."

"Did you ever meet any of his relatives or go to his house?"

"No, there was never an invitation."

"We understand that your neighbor, Kyria Stathakos, and others are a big help to you right now. Officer Vatis said she is willing to assist if you need anything. Here is our card; I have put both phones on it. If something comes up, or you think of something, please give either of us a call."

"Everyone has been so kind, especially Officer Vatis. She left her card and wrote a quotation of sympathy that made me feel so much better."

Geró smiled at the mention of his quotation.

* * * * * * * *

"I don't think she approved of Fotis Grigoris," said Pidalios as he shut his car door.

"Do you blame her?" came the answer from the back. "We have to agree. He has done nothing to ease her pain, nor has he been helpful in our investigation." As they approached the village center, "Look, speak of the devil, there's his truck. He's probably in that hardware store. Let's wait until he comes out."

"How do you know it's his truck?" Pidalios pulled over and parked nearby so they could see.

"The name Grigoris is on it in big, bold letters with a design."

When they saw him exit the store and walk to the back of his truck, they got out and approached him. He didn't see them until he finished putting his purchases into the truck bed, and he was surprised. "What are you two doing, following me?"

"Now why would we do that, Mr. GRIGORAKIS?" said Geró.

"Grigoris, remember? You didn't stop here in Kaminia to say hello."

"Yes, we did. We visited with Kyria Politis. Have you?"

"Not yet. I wanted to give her time to grieve; then I'll call on her. Better yet, I'll see her at his funeral on Tuesday. The morgue has released his body for burial."

"That would be an appropriate gesture. I do have a question for you though."

Looking resentful, he crossed his arms over his chest, "Give it your best shot."

"You said you tripped."

"What are you talking about?"

"Up on the mountain when you shot your friend."

"I did trip, and the shot was accidental."

"Before or after the noise?"

"What noise?"

"That's odd you don't remember. A shepherd up there says there were two shots fired in succession."

"That's right. I heard a shot. It made me react. I tripped on the tangled weeds, and that's when I shot my buddy—the gun went off. I have said it so many times. I didn't mean it. Was it Vras' gun that fired?"

"We don't know yet," said Pidalios. "We'll keep you informed."

They walked to the car. He still stood there and watched as they drove away.

"What a fake!" said Pidalios. 'He wanted to give her time to grieve,' my ass."

"I noticed he kept rubbing his face with his hand. I get the impression his attitude and body language show he is worried about something. We must get the gun evidence. When the captain returns Friday, we'll ask to speak to their weapons expert and get access to any shell casings or hulls, slugs and the two guns used at the scene. Maybe that evidence will assist in a conclusion."

"Only the police have access to all of that. In fact, didn't John tell us that twice Grigoris has asked if he can have his gun back? Could be that's what he's upset about," said Pidalios.

"Until Friday we will work on that farmer's case against the Bank of Sparti—as boring as it is. And, I will call the doctor. He did not call us.

"If you want to join Thia and me for some of that lamb and noodles later, you are welcome. Call my sister Paraskevi and tell her you won't be home for supper. She can either join us, or Irini will send some home for her. She actually complimented Irini's Greek cooking skills the last time she ate with us. It only took Irini thirty years of practice." He laughed.

Chapter 10

The phone rang at the detective agency and Geró picked up. "Hello, this is Dr. Veloutis. I am the resident physician working with Dr. Karis. I think we met at the hospital last week. Dr. Karis asked me to call you, and I have also forwarded a copy of this report to the captain."

"I was just about to call the doctor— excellent. Is he there?"

"He is very busy at the moment and can't be disturbed, but he asked that I call you with the final results from the post mortem examination of Vrasithas Politis, the dead hunter."

Karis is probably out for a cigarette, Geró thought, but he responded with, "I'm all ears."

"Dr. Karis said you had concerns about the angle of entry. The shot entered through the upper back on an at least forty-five degree angle, and the irregular fragments from it caused severe tissue damage in the neck and upper back by creating an avulsed wound in the upper right quadrant. That caused Politis' death from massive internal hemorrhaging. I am also aware that you were previously informed that he was a healthy person with no apparent disease of any kind."

The response was "By avulsed wound you are saying that a tearing away led to the bleeding? In the upper right side of the back—above the 'chicken wing?'"

Dr. Veloutis laughed aloud at the 'non medical' term used. "That is right, the chicken wing. In line with Greece's hunting regulations, the shot was from a smooth bore rifle, twelve gauge."

"At least the killer used the correct weapon," said Geró.

Once again Dr. Veloutis burst out laughing. "You're a very funny man, sir, but I may get into trouble for all this merriment in the morgue. Is there anything else you need information or results about?"

"If I do, I know who to call. Thank you." As he was hanging up, he could hear more snickering.

Pidalios walked in, and Geró repeated what he had just been told. "I said that at the beginning, about the gun being shot on an angle. It seems to be true. How tall do you think Fotis is?"

Pidalios replied, "If I had to guess, I would say five ten or less."

"At the post mortem they said that Vrasithas Politis was five feet nine inches. Keeping that in mind, I'd have to assume that, if Grigoris shot him, he held the gun over his head and pointed it down. Since the hunter has to use two hands to hold the shotgun, that would be a tough stance. It doesn't make any sense unless we have the wrong height of each man…"

"…or unless he was standing on a rock or step stool, and we didn't find either at the scene." Pidalios smirked.

"The other question to ask Friday, when we speak to the captain, is the brand of carabina (gun) used by each man on that hunt. I do recall that Fotis was armed with a Browning because he kept talking about that damn shotgun when leaving the interview that first day. He actually asked to take it home with him."

"I think I dislike him so much because of his arrogance. I want to know now if he followed all regulations for hunting here in Greece. We know he's over eighteen and, since he was born here, he's a citizen, but did he apply for a license and get permission to hunt for wild boar. They are rarely seen— almost extinct in the mountains here."

"True, wild boar and woodcock were very often hunted for years. Recently they have been seen more, and it is considered a real treasure to bag one. Those deadly horns are dangerous, and they are huge, ugly monsters."

"Did you read they have been known to grow six to eight feet in length, Thio?"

"Not those around here I hope."

"Pidalios answered his phone. 'Legate?' Good news, sergeant. 9:00 a. m.? Tell the captain we'll be there." He turned to his partner. "You heard? The captain at 9, okay?"

"I'm anxious to see him."

The cell phone sounded again. "Hey, Thia. That's all right. We were just discussing tall pigs." He cracked up at her response and said, "Not the women I date. Neh, he's right here. Take care." He handed his cell to his uncle and remarked, "funny woman you married."

Looking quizzically at him, Geró took the phone. "Irinimou, what's up?"

"Geró, I'm sorry to bother you, but I don't want you to make plans for the weekend because George and Rani are coming." She sounded so pleased.

George and Urania (Rani) had been their friends since they lived in New York. Before Irini met Geró, he worked for George in his high end restaurant on Madison Ave. Since both men were Greek and got along well, the two friends became four friends, wives included. Although Irini and Geró lived here permanently, they still got together with their friends annually when George and Rani spent several months in their home in Thessaloniki in northern Greece. It was a perfect place for rest and a respite from NYC.

"Great news. When are they arriving? Should I make reservations at a hotel for them?"

"No, Rani said they heard about the Menelaion. I told her how beautiful the place is and that we can have such a good lunch there on Saturday.

"Our treat. Did he make reservations?"

"All done," Irini said. "We'll talk later."

The meeting with the captain was set, and they were there on time to have coffee with him. "How was Athens, John? Good meeting?"

"Frankly, a long ride to sit with the bureaucrats, and I didn't learn anything except new regulations and that there is no money available for my budget. I'm glad to be back."

They explained all their activity over the last few days and Geró explained what Dr. Veloutis said about the angle of entry of the wound. John told them, "There are methods with lasers that can determine the line of fire—bullet trajectory analysis. Experts in that are only a few, at least in these surroundings. You did take photos at the scene, didn't you? because Goovis didn't." He looked at Pidalios.

"I learned the art of detection from my uncle. The first thing he berated me about was my lack of evidence bags; the second was to photograph the crime scene in its entirety."

"Excellent, because if we have pictures of spent casings that were marked with placards there, and pictures or drawings of objects found at the scene, we can use a simple procedure called 'Stringing,' which I am not familiar with. Maybe the lab guys…."

"John," asked Geró, is it okay with you if we call Thodoris and Taki to come to do this 'Stringing' as you said. We can call them now and arrange it—that's if they know how it's done."

"Be my guest," said John.

"I'll call," said Pidalios. He stepped out to do just that. When he came back in ten minutes later to interrupt a jovial conversation, he had everything set up. "Good news. Thodoris said they just so happen to be available to be here tomorrow. They'll bring their minivan, fully equipped, and arrive around eleven. I said they can meet me up there. Of course, you two are welcome."

"I can not be there," said Geró to the captain. Irini just called to tell me our American-Greek friends are arriving in the early afternoon."

"You are excused, my friend," said Sakalidis. "I must be there to accompany our evidence, the shotguns. So, count me in. Before you go Pidalios, are you sure they have all the necessary equipment?"

"If it's not in that minivan, it doesn't exist," Geró told him. "Pidalios will fill me in after you experts have reached all possible conclusions."

"Let's get to the actual weapons," said the captain. "Fotis Grigoris carried a new, expensive 1994 Browning, ballistic optimizing system A-Bolt Two, hunter-Euro Bolt 12 gauge. A beauty! He saved his drachmas for that one. Vrasithas Politis, the novice, carried a used 1990 Remington Model 870, 12 gauge. It's been around since the 1950s; yet, it is the most trusted, smoothest pump shotgun."

"The choice of weapons by each man seems to fit their natures," observed Geró.

Pidalios silently marveled at his Thio's observations, but he said, "Did they both have special permission and licenses?"

"They had followed the rules, and both men had their licenses clearly carried outside on their jackets."

Geró stood. They had taken too much time already. "Thanks, John, and I will talk to you soon."

"Pidalios said, "All of us will meet on Tayegatos in the morning. Thank you."

"I am grateful to both of you," said their friend, Capt. John Sakalidis. "I don't have the manpower or the money to solve this on our own."

Chapter 11

All interested parties arrived earlier than the set time to meet up at the gully. As Pidalios pulled up, he realized he arrived with the birds but was still last. He saw the Tripoli lab minivan, doors open, and the captain's car parked next to it. He walked down to the crime scene with his evidence and all the containers of coffee he brought.

"Kali mera, everybody. I'm not late, but, since you are all early, I guess I'm late. So, I brought coffee and donuts." He passed it out, and the captain thanked him, saying, "It's chilly up here in the morning." The others nodded as they chewed on donuts, and Pidalios drank his iced coffee through a straw and took out the official scene photos to give to Thodoris and Taki, who were authorized by the Astynomia ΔΕΕ, the forensic division.

Sgt. Goovis and a patrol officer had strung crime scene tape everywhere and stood watch so curious hunters would not interfere. All was prepared. First they examined the shotguns and checked the photos. Taki had made sketches from the copies Pidalios sent. These were helpful in spotting actual crime scene trees and rocks.

The markings, placed to show where the body had rested and approximate position of the head, neck and back, were important to the results of the 'Stringing.' This test, known to have a few shortcomings, could still prove the line of bullet travel up to ninety percent. Regular string drooped and sagged, so they were using strong synthetic string. The lab men had chosen it over hollow aluminum rods or wooden dowels to show the path to Politis' back. "With a bigger budget we could use an inclinometer, a directional compass, or a laser pointer," said Thodoris.

"You guys are so adept at forensic testing; your methods will get the job done," said the captain.

Taki held Vrasithas Politis' Remington in the spot marked on the sketch. Sgt. Goovis, of similar height, was called down from his post to hold Grigoris' Browning and face Politis' back. The obvious result was that Grigoris, using that gun, did not stand in that place and shoot his friend. Did he shoot from another place and come down afterward to call the police and bawl? possibly?

Pidalios and Sakalidis agreed that the rock and bushes, jutting out up there, were the same that Tsengos, the shepherd, said he saw when the woman hurried away. Now it was marked with a symbol on the sketch, and they helped Thodoris carry the shotguns and equipment up there. Taki would stay down to check the path the bullet took.

The rock and bush were exactly as drawn. The view down to the body was clear and definitely within range of the weapon. Before they climbed back down, Sakalidis and Pidalios scrupulously checked all around for anything that was missed evidence.

Thodoris waited for them to get out of his way before he waved to Taki that he was now beginning the 'Stringing' experiment to see if the shotgun slug could have killed Politis from up here.

At the end of the day, it was proven that the fatal shot had been fired from the top, not the ground. The lab would send a formal report on video, as well as a printed form, but they informed the captain and Pidalios what they had temporarily concluded. Taki, on the ground had also discovered a slug far ahead, embedded in a rock.

"When we finish our work on all of this," said Thodoris, "we'll be in touch as soon as possible." The forensic team drove off slowly.

Pidalios yelled out, "No more donuts until you also get results out of the hair, red bow, κτλ [ktl-etcetera]." He shook hands with all the others, got in his car and led the slow parade down the mountain. At the bottom he pulled over and called his Thio to fill him in on the successful morning findings.

"Sorry I couldn't be there, but you did a great job. I know because the captain just told me."

"Were you checking up on me?" Pidalios laughed.

"He called me. Now I have to go. Irini is urging me to leave to meet Rani and George. If you would like to see them again, we will be at the Menelaion for the rest of the afternoon and probably Anavryti for dinner later."

"I'll try. First I have to see to all the work you left to take care of at the office before you were going to spas and resorts."

"I got this from an unknown source: 'When I count my blessings, I count you twice.'"

"Aw, thank you, Thio," and he closed the phone.

Chapter 12

Geró and Irini went into the lobby of the Menelaion Hotel and inquired if their friends had arrived. The receptionist pointed to the dining room, and, when they looked, George was beckoning to them from a table.

"Giorgo, Rani," Geró hugged and kissed them on both cheeks.

Irini stepped right in and repeated the warm greeting. "I am always amazed when we meet. No couple looks as great as you. I must say it's becoming boring." They all chuckled at her remark.

"I can say the same about you two," George used all his charm.

"Keep it up, ψεύτης [pseftis-liar]." said Irini.

"Irini, your Greek gets better all the time," said Rani. "Your description of my husband is spot on. Now, I suggest we all stop complimenting each other and have lunch. I'm hungry after the long trip."

"Don't eat too much because dinner is on us in one of our most scenic places, up in

Anavryti at the top of Mt. Tayegatos," said Geró.

"If I remember, you have relatives from there, neh?" asked George.

"My grandfather was born there, and my cousin Panagiotis, you know, from New York, Giorgo."

Irini interrupted, "Anyhow, we thought we would take you up there for dinner tonight to our favorite place, 'Amarantos'—named for the flower Amaranth that thrives up there.

"Amarantos means immortal, unfading, doesn't it?" added Rani. What a great name for a restaurant; George, maybe you and Panagiotis, your partner, should rename yours."

"It's owned by a man named Peter Soumakis, great guy. Every year on my name day, Irini throws me a dinner party there and invites relatives and everyone we're close to from here and friends from several countries who happen to be visiting in July. Peter sets a very long and bountiful table for about twenty or so, looking out over the mountain, and his wife, Marina cooks platter after bowl of the most delicious Greek dishes, and we sit, talk and admire the scenic beauty from up there. If you're interested, we'll pick you up about 7."

"We will look forward to it," said George. "It sounds great after lunch and a good nap, right Rani?"

"Perfect," she said as Lena, their server, approached the table. Lena had come to Greece from Russia. Her husband was one of the owners of this hotel, and she had known Geró and Irini for years.

As she turned over the water and wine glasses, she said hello to their friends. Geró introduced Rani and George and explained where they were from in Greece, but that he also owned a restaurant in Manhattan, where they had their main residence. "New York, the big apple; it is my dream to go there." That led to more conversation as she gave each of them a menu and poured the water. "I'm so sorry to be taking your time. I will let you read the menu, and I'll be back shortly."

"How long has she lived here?" asked George. Her Greek is excellent."

"She's been here a long time. Her son is about twenty, I think," said Irini,
and I think I know what I want: κορφαδες [cor fath es-stuffed zucchini flowers].

"That sounds good to me too," said Rani.

"Not me, said Geró, "I'll take the fattening makaronatha with lots of cheese. Give us a horiatiki salata (village salad). Okay with everyone?"

"Κοτόπουλο [ko toe poo lo-chicken] for me, and how about some graviera cheese for all of us," said George. "Wine?" Everyone said no, so he remarked, "tonight, on us." Then the conversation never waned among these old friends as they enjoyed lunch.

"Are you here for the weekend only?" asked Irini.

"Yes, we'll leave Sunday afternoon to get back to Thessaloniki reasonably late. We booked for New York on the 11th," said Rani.

"I can understand that," Irini said. "There is no place like the city for Thanksgiving and Christmas—the magnificent tree in Rockefeller Center, the department stores' window decorations. Ah, I miss all of it."

Rani said, "Maybe you should visit during the holidays."

"That would be terrific," Geró spoke up, "but Pidalios and I are working on a tragic murder case with the Astynomia that took place on the first day of a wild boar hunt up on the mountain."

"They still hunt up there?" asked George.

"Neh, and it just happened on the first day of hunting season, so I'm sure it won't be solved for a while. One man shot his friend in the back with a shotgun."

"And it was murder? friends? I thought you were going to say a husband did away with his yineka (wife);" he looked at beautiful Rani.

"Or the reverse," she smirked.

The four went on to share news of the past year—more pleasant than just the usual 'who's related to whom,' and what distant old person died in their family at 98. Irini made them laugh as she told them the story of Geró stealing. "No, not Geró," said Rani.

"He did. The place was a barely surviving supermarket that I stopped at on our way home from Gytheion. After we filled our cart and went to the checkout, he did his usual 'bagging' because he thinks no one does it better. I saw the clerk look strangely at him, and he said something to her like 'got it all' or 'all done'— didn't really hear.

"She was young and didn't say anything else, and I took the change. When we got into the car, I said to him, 'What did you buy? It was so heavy.' Everything was in the trunk, and I drove off. When I was unpacking the many bags, I discovered that one contained only a giant roll of paper towels. Geró, I called out. Why is this here? I never buy this; it's extremely thin junk."

"'It was at the end of the counter, so I bagged it,'" he told me.

"I didn't buy it. You stole it! Now I realize why the cashier looked at you like that. Oh, my God, I'm married to a thief. We must take it back."

"Twenty some kilometers at this time of night. Are you crazy? I'll stop in and pay for it the next time we're going by."

Rani and George stopped laughing, and he said, "The famous detective—a common thief!"

"The best kind, though," joked Geró.

The rest of the lunch went on in this light, humorous way, and their guests agreed to be picked up at seven that night.

That evening up in Anavryti, George and Rani marveled at the tiny but historic village and the breathtaking scenery. When they walked to the restaurant, Pidalios was already standing next to their table to greet them.

"How great to see you both again."

"And you too. You look healthy, in great shape," said George. "Your Thio keeps you running, I see."

"In restaurants you call the second a sous chef, right. In the detective business I'm the go-fer."

"Poor you," said Geró.

It was a spectacular evening up there under the sky, and dinner tasted better than it would anywhere else—probably because of the setting. Evening was closing in when Pidalios told the story of eating with his Thia and Thio and a few others one night outside as it was getting dark. "The dinner plates had been turned upside down on the tablecloth. It was quite dim. My Thio took the first platter and scooped some of the food onto the still overturned base of his plate. All eyes opened wide and looked at each other. No one dared laugh, at least not at that moment. We all just turned our plates right side up as Thia Irini signaled quietly for the waiter to bring Thio a clean plate."

"Don't say a word," threatened Geró. "I was sitting under an overhang and did not see the plate in that position, you know, dim candles and all."

George burst with laughter and so did everyone else, including the highly intelligent Geró Peerooney. George said, "This was such a great day, especially among dear friends." They all agreed.

Chapter 13

After a late breakfast Sunday morning at IL Posto in the Plateia, Rani and George left for home. As they walked to their apartment, enjoying the sunny morning with the sound of church bells providing background, Geró said, "'Friends are those rare people who ask how we are and then wait to hear the answer.' I don't know who he is, but an American athlete/sportscaster, named Cunningham said it, and i think it truly defines friendship."

"Also, it is a pleasure to see friends who never overstay," Irini added to that wisdom.

Monday morning Pidalios gave him the details of the Mt. Tayegatos 'forensic clinic' with the Astynomia and their lab friends last Friday. "You were right again, Thio, when you said you thought the case rested on the angle of entry of the slug. The Stringing test proved Politis was killed with a slug from up above the chasm, canyon, gulch, abyss, or whatever the hell it's called."

"I'm not sure myself, but I must say your knowledge of synonyms is much better. Call the lab and find out if they will have any hints or evidence—say Wednesday? early in the day. Remember we have a funeral to attend tomorrow morning. However, my learned partner, once again, before that sad ceremony we shall have to go to Kaminia.

"To talk with Mavrogenis?"

"Always that, but this time to check that old house of the shamed daughter, Maria. I want to pick up something there," said Geró, "and I don't think we should be snooping around on the day of the funeral."

"If it's something important, we can take a ride there now."

"It's the threadbare old blanket left there by the hearth, and please bring a very large evidence bag for it. Maybe T& T can test it."

"You know, Thio, they say it is a sign of early dementia when a person repeats himself. I always have all sized bags in my trunk," he said repetitiously, "but what if it belongs to someone?"

"Did you see its condition; it's a ragged old thing, useful maybe but shabby."

"I have my illegal picks in the car in case there's a lock on the door."

"For what?" Let's go now."

Kaminia was a quiet horio, and no one questioned when they parked a ways down from the Katsouris house. They knocked and called out anyhow, but after no response, Pidalios did not need his picks. Just a moderate push on the old door swung it in. The cover was still rolled up on the floor, and he took it and labeled it for evidence. They didn't want to leave any prints from hands or feet, and they departed.

Pidalios slowly drove by Mavrogenis' house, but the old gentleman was absent from his usual place. They decided that he most definitely would be at the funeral in the morning, so they drove off. "Why did you want that old rag?" asked Pidalios.

"I want the lab to test it."

"For what?"

"Scent."

"You mean odor? like from a sweaty body?"

"There is probably that from many bodies who used it. No, it's called scent evidence— human scent from an object touched. You wore gloves when you bagged it; I think I saw that."

"Would I ever touch anything especially that, without gloves?"

"No, but the team will explain odorology and scent evidence to us on Wednesday when we go to Tripoli. Listen, let me get off here. Then you can have the open road to yourself to smoke. We'll see you tomorrow at the funeral."

"Don't you want to be picked up?"

"Thank you, no, Thia will want to go, I'm sure, so she'll drive."

"She didn't know the deceased."

"She will wish to observe the people and look for possible suspects."

"See you there." Geró saw the trail of exhaled cigarette smoke leaving the open window as the car drove off.

Chapter 14

Tuesday morning at 10:00 people were solemnly entering the small church in Kaminia when Irini parked their car. She pointed out her nephew who, standing away from the entrance, had joined other men for their last few puffs. She exited the driver's side as Geró climbed out of the front passenger seat to go to Pidalios.

She walked up and greeted her nephew. "Did you just arrive?" she asked.

"About ten minutes ago, Thia. Lovely suit that is." He admired his aunt's black pin-striped suit that she had purchased in Athens recently. "Did you really want to come here?" he said to her as he reached to shake his uncle's hand.

"I told Thio I would drive him."

"Thank you for liking my suit and offering to drive, ανιψιόςμου [ah neep cee os mou-my nephew]. I was shocked by the tragedy of this death, and frankly I also hope to meet Mavrogenis, but I go where your uncle goes on formal and somber occasions."

"Plus, he is always grateful for your powers of observation," Pidalios glanced at his uncle as he added, "since he is aging."

The three entered and sat near the back of the church next to Capt. Sakalidis. The young widow with her two children entering, going up front and standing to 'welcome the deceased' as the procession of priests and the coffin entered, made Irini grip Geró's arm. They observed the mournful procession.

The church filled with friends, villagers and the curious. During the Mass Pidalios whispered that Fotis Grigoris had come in but stood close to the door. "At least he showed up."

"I'm sure he is full of sadness and guilt," said Irini.

"He is not winning any popularity contests," Geró uttered. When the Mass was over, he said, "Let's go up on the altar and pay our final respects to Vrasithas before they close the coffin."

Over the years Irini had been transformed into what she referred to as nearly totally Greek. The one cultural and religious difference that still put her off was the practice that she could barely endure. The body lay in an open coffin up on the altar during the entire Mass, and after all religious blessings, prayers and symbolism had been finalized by the priest, the grieving family was forced, not only to stand in a receiving line and listen to solemn condolences but also being grabbed, bear-hugged, kissed by tear-stained, make up streaked or unshaven faces of despondency. Those who had been on the altar to touch, kiss or pray over the deceased, delivered these avowals. It took such a protracted amount of time, not only because of long lines, but also because it seemed that some mourners had to prove their extreme degree of bereavement for all to hear and see.

Irini remembered a funeral parlor visit in America where an old man in a wheel chair came in late in the evening and began screeching the name of the man in the coffin. 'Oh, God, no. Don't take my best friend.' It turned out that the invalid knew the deceased only because he stopped in at his coffee shop about once a month.

Geró introduced his wife to Katina Politis and her children and to the priest, Dr. Matritis from Kaminia, Sgt. Vatis and Kyrios Mavrogenis who stood next to the helpful neighbor, Kyria Stathakos. Irini, not wanting to overstep her place, removed herself from the widow's friends and stood by John Sakalidis and spoke briefly to Mavrogenis. She and Geró left soon after because they considered the service in the church graveyard as private, and they would also not go to the after service luncheon that Kyria Stathakos told them was presented in the house for everyone.

As they drove from the church, Irini told her husband that Mavrogenis said he would be pleased if she stopped in at any time.

"So, my dear wife, you always get your way."

"Don't berate me, Geró. I asked you twice if we could stop to speak with him, Glika and all, and you put me off, so I politely brought it up to him."

"I guess I'm not the only man who can't resist you. More importantly, did you happen to see anything or anybody who was acting suspiciously?"

"I didn't. I was totally absorbed in watching the grieving widow and how she kept hugging her children to her. What a sad, sad story, and she is too young."

"The good people in the village are supporting her and the children, and hopefully we will reach a resolution about his tragic death."

Geró left Irini at their apartment. She said she wanted to write her thoughts about this day and that village. Possibly the plaintive journal entry would be material for her next book.

Her husband walked down to the office, and, as he unlocked the door, he heard the phone ringing. "Detective agency…"

"…I know that. Listen, Thio, Taki called as I was leaving the church. He said the slug, embedded in the rock up there, was from a 1990 Remington-model 870, 12 gauge shotgun."

"That was Vrasithas Politis' gun, right? I'm surprised it could be examined—that it wasn't shattered."

"Now, here's the best part. All this time we thought the slug, found ahead on the ground, was his and that he fired it involuntarily when he was hit. That one was from a 1994 Browning Euro Bolt, 12 gauge."

"Fotis Grigoris' gun?"

"That's a match. He missed Vrasithas. He's not the killer. He probably did trip on those twisted weeds on the ground as he told us."

"Are T & T going to do further tests? Recheck the slugs?"

"Definitely, and the one that killed Politis was from another Browning, made in Belgium in the 1970s."

"Now we know that the Stringing test worked, the killer was up near the rock. Great work!"

"Thank you, Thio."

"I meant that for our lab buddies. I will call them after I call Sakalidis." Geró did that, and, when he called T & T to thank them, he got a seminar on shotguns, shells, slugs and how shell casings can be compared to samples fired from a suspect gun. They would have gone on, but he told them they were masters of analysis and he treasured their assistance in solving this murder. He said that when they had more on the smudged red bow or saliva, hair and fingerprints on the Fisherman's Friend box, he would gift them with something for their lab.

"We'll keep at it," Thodoris said. "It's what we do," Taki chimed in.

Chapter 15

"Geró, while you were out detecting all day, I decided to do a little study of my own about perfumes. You and Pidalios are waiting for reports on odors and items they cling to even after a period of time has passed. Odorology is a new study.

I did some research into 'parfum' creators of the world and their tests of fixatives. I checked the internet, and the bowels of the library." He raised an eyebrow in her direction.

"You know, the stored books, out of date and in the basements, here and in surrounding libraries. There were remnants of an unbound lecture on perfumes, flower farming and methods of obtaining 'odours' of plants. This lecture had been delivered before the Royal Horticultural Society by a person named G.W. Plesse in 1865. It was in poor, yellowing page shape, but it was fascinating—from the parts I could read.

"For example: agar—its origin is red seaweed."

"Not green? or brown?"

"Just red. And wait until you hear this one. Castoreum is an oily cream, found in the sac of a beaver. Each exquisite scent generally comes from a source that you would not believe. Musk, a haunting fragrance, comes from the deer in the Himalayas."

"That is incredible. No wonder it is so costly. They have to climb all the way up there to get it."

She ignored that and continued. "The scent of the sea—the main component of ambergris is found in sperm whales. It is part of the 1965 scent of Nina Ricci. Chanel and Marcel Rochas label products blend vanilla with phenyl propanoids…"

"Whatever they are."

"…to make their spicy floral scents. They give a pleasant, sweet and spicy scent even though they are chemical compounds."

Looking at his wife and impressed but teasing her, he came back with, "I know one.

I'll bet rosy floral perfumes are made from rose oil."

"Since you are not interested in the origin of scents, I will give you more informative, everyday facts. Ninety percent of women use perfume, and sixty percent of men use scent of some type. Not to get too French on you, in Lyon at the Centre de Recherche en Neurosciences, work is being done on new methods of odorology in scent evidence. They put an odor on sterile pads in jars, and dogs sniff and search. Unless an area has been burned, such as at a murder scene, human scent from an object someone has worn—an example: perfume on a scarf or coat will lead to a match. It can remain there for weeks. One must take in all environmental factors, though, such as wind, temperature, humidity and terrain. Scent will also adhere to objects like cigarette butts, match books and styrofoam cups."

"Hair? bows? cough drop boxes? by any chance?"

"I would assume so," she answered. "I got so obsessed with this research."

"Tell me more. I am paying attention."

"Animals have amazing ability to smell. German shepherds are best at scent trails; yet, bloodhounds are quite remarkable themselves."

"Bloodhounds are used for the hunt in England."

"Listen to this outstanding fact. A sheep dog has two hundred million olfactory cells compared to six to ten million in humans. The sheep dog smells forty to one thousand times better than humans."

"No wonder they are so valuable to my cousin, the chopanis. I'll call Pidalios and ask him if the lab has our possible scent evidence still sealed."

"If it is in a bag, they probably knew to freeze it, and it would then still be okay. I read that frozen evidence can be re-activated, when frozen, after fifteen or so minutes."

"You certainly are voluble today, Irinimou. Is there more info you can offer toward my education? If not, let me call Pidalios about that lab evidence—hopefully frozen." He got up and went to use the phone, marveling at having such an intelligent, resourceful wife. He recalled an unknown source quote that was apt, but he did it silently.

"Some people arrive and make such a beautiful impact on your life, you can barely remember what life was like without them."

Chapter 16

The day they moved from their New York apartment, they did not use a moving company because of low funds and meager furnishings that were left after they sold or gave away the rest. Two friends promised to come to help them move boxes and bags into a rental van. Only her Greek tutor from NYU showed up. Irini was going through some turmoil. Leaving family and friends to move to a foreign country was causing her some pain.

She had only to clear the everyday dishes from the kitchen cabinets. Every other necessary thing had been packed. Irini opened the cabinet door, and right in front of her face, lying on its back on top of a white plate, was a large, dead cockroach. She slammed the door shut and announced, "Forget the dinnerware. Every thing stays here." That was after she screamed. In three years of residence there, she had never before spotted a roach. Irini had her fears: heights, mice and cockroaches. Snakes were a close runner up.

Whenever she tried to face these life long fears, she failed. In Greece she would overcome much of her fear of heights with a lot of help for five years.

It took even longer than that for her to become an independent woman, but she had done it very well. She warmed to the culture, cherished Geró's family and became an expert at not being overly sensitive to criticism from those who expressed their opinion and spread gossip. Didn't Euripides say, "Judge a tree by its fruit, not its leaves."

Geró supported her, even in public places. They joined some acquaintances one afternoon at a cafe in the plateia. After introductions all around, one man—a Greek visitor from Canada, became combative towards her when he learned she was an American. His effrontery about everything American, directed at her at least three times, outraged her. She finally had enough and came back with, "What a man! You are capable of multiple sarcasms." She stood, said goodbye as several people were still laughing at him, and she walked off.

Later Geró caught up with her at a store and said, "I watched your anger grow as he made ridiculous anti-America statements, but you got him with that final blow. How did you come up with that quote? Was it from a book or a movie?"

"I'm not sure where. Maybe TV? His onslaught of sarcastic remarks could not be brushed aside. I knew you would not want to intervene. He is a feckless, ignorant moron, and I could not sit there any longer."

"None of the others blamed you."

"Thank you for that, and thank you for allowing me to let him have it."

"An anonymous quote that fits is 'The real power of a man is the size of the smile of the woman sitting next to him.' You are a wonderful wife. Please keep on being the independent woman who pleases me."

They said no more on the subject, but they got in the car and Irini drove them the many kilometers to Valtaki Cove for that dinner he had promised a couple of weeks ago.

The owner greeted them warmly and once again pointed to one of Irini's books: "Murder at Valtaki Cove." It was proudly displayed because of a photo of the beach as well as one shot of her and Pidalios, taken in this restaurant, that appeared in the book.

Chapter 17

During the next week a report was faxed from the lab to the agency and the police. It stated that the scent on the tangle of dark brown hair matched that on the old, tattered blanket from the Katsouris house in Kaminia. The second revelation was that the smudge on the red bow was from gun oil. It had a partial print that was not up to the regulations of discovery to use as evidence.

Thodoris included a personal note: "We are doing a DNA test on the saliva from the foil inside the Fisherman's Friend cough drop box. We will fax ASAP if more is learned."

Geró called the lab and was included in a conference call. "Morning you two. Thank you for the information thus far. We appreciate everything. I do have an opinion as to how saliva was found on the inner foil pack."

"We discussed that and concluded that the murderer used fingertips coated with moisture from the tongue to open the packet."

"I'm sure you are correct," said Geró. "How many times have I tried to open a plastic bag in a produce department, or a foil inner pack that instructs me to 'pull edges to open.' Instead I licked my fingers—worked every time."

Taki said, "The shooter had to ready the shotgun and probably didn't want to be heard during his coughing and tried to pull…"

"…instead tried to use his teeth to break the foil pouch, and he inadvertently left a saliva trace. What do you think of that?" Geró offered.

"Could be the answer," said Taki. Also, we have been discussing the footprint, pointing down from up there. Our best guess is that the killer, trying to get off an accurate shot, leaned into it. The front foot slipped off the edge. To maintain balance he dug in his heel. That's why the back of the print has more depth in the cast you took at the scene."

"We're getting closer. I hate to ask this, but do you have any idea what the brand name of that scent is?"

"No, but we think it is a scent that a woman would choose. We have charts from many Paris parfumeries and are in contact. We will get a sample to them. Since it is a police matter, they cooperate, and we will get back to you as quickly as we can."

"Ευχαριστώ [ef har ee sto-thank you]."

"No thanks needed. Is there any other thing at the moment?"

"We'll be in touch." Geró hung up.

Within that same week Pidalios got a call on his cell phone from Taki. "Don't you two take naps?" he answered.

"We don't have time for that, so we just lock the door and keep working. It bothered me the first month, but once you get out of that habit, you don't miss it. Besides, with everything else closed, we are not interrupted. Maybe you're getting old, Pidalios."

"Even tourists love our afternoon nap tradition. Never mind that. Is there any news for us?"

"Thodoris got an answer for us from an odorology lab. The perfume was originally made in France. It is called Pani Walewska by Miraculum. It is very popular because it's a symbol of femininity, floral-chypre."

"Wait. How do you spell that last word?"

"C-H-Y-P-R-E."

"What is that?"

"I checked. It is a concept of perfumes-from several scents of the eight major families of smells. The top person in each perfume lab is called 'nose.' Isn't that fitting?"

"I think it is."

"We can't go any further other than the brand name."

"You did great, and my Thia can check whatever we need. Recently she has been studying perfumes and how they are made."

"Great!" He then recited the list of sources for the perfume industry, and the call was ended.

Pidalios' next call was to report to Geró. Irini answered that call. She made note of everything he learned from the lab and promised an intense investigation into the art of making perfume. She wasn't sure her husband wouldn't consider her study an interference, but he surprised her by being grateful.

When he left the apartment, she got right to it. Her discoveries became more interesting. Pani Walewska was originally made in Paris. Now it was made by Miraculum in other countries. The process succeeds using chypre and the major families of scents, such as citrus, floral, Oriental (feminine), Oriental (masculine), aromatics and woody masculine. Synthetic chemicals are used to emulate the scent. A blending of ingredients to create that scent. Common ingredients are rose petals, myrrh, frankincense, jasmine, oak moss, sandalwood, vanilla and citron.

The most important person, working on the mix is called 'nose' because that person is responsible for blending the ingredients to create the product. Eau de perfume lasts longer and costs more, and eau de toilette is suitable for everyday.

Irini was amazed to discover that the most expensive perfumes in the world cost as much as one million an ounce. These costs had nothing to do with her report, but she wanted to note the prices. Caron Poivre was blended in 1954—made to mark the fiftieth anniversary of the House of Caron. It cost $1,000 then. Chanel Grand Extract #5 in 1921 sold for $4,200 US dollars. Baccarat blended a perfume a few years ago that cost $6,800. Clive Christian No.1 Imperial Majesty, meant to conjure up images of Aphrodite, goddess of beauty and love, sold for $12,750 dollars.

Irini set this information aside, just for Geró's eyes, as she thought of the time he bought her favorite perfume 'Floris,' in London at Selfridges for $175. Now she could no longer buy her favorite discontinued scent. She was not upset over this because here in Sparta during several hot months perfume was rarely used. It drew 'koonoopies-mosquitos' to feast on women. How her life had changed over these years here! When they lived in New York, she would lightly spray the air above her hair and quickly step under it. That's all it took. No matter where she went, such as stepping into an elevator, someone was bound to say, 'I smell the scent of carnations.' She would smile and stay quiet, experiencing what a beautiful scent could create.

She reported her findings to her husband that night, and he said, "So, we know we have a match from her hair and the blanket, but how do we use this to find her."

"How many women can afford such perfumes? Maybe they have their clients' names, or addresses—at least the stores that sell them."

"That's a good thought, but would a woman of wealth be sleeping on a ratty blanket in Kaminia. Possibly you have saved us a few steps, Irinimou.

Chapter 18

Geró sat at his desk in the office. He had been here for more than two hours. A legal pad was in front of him, and he was going over the list he called 'what now?' During the night some minor thought interrupted his sleep. He knew he had to get out of bed; he would not be able to go back to sleep, so he dressed and came here. Pidalios would be arriving soon, and they would check the list and decide on their plan of action in solving this case. If Pidalios didn't bring his everyday iced coffee, Geró had made enough hot coffee for both of them.

The door opened and with a pleasant greeting, Pidalios entered. "Morning, Thio." He put two bags, containing fried bread, on the table.

"I've been here quite a while, and, as you can see, I made a long list to discuss. Oh, and thanks for the breakfast."

The two men went down the list and added these items: blood found in the soil taken from up above the crime scene, and a ride back to

Kaminia to check the Katsouris house for any missed evidence.

"I also have a call to make," said Geró.

"To?"

"Sam."

"Great idea. If anyone can help, he can. First, may I suggest a ride to Kaminia. The time difference in Egypt must be a consideration." He looked at his watch. "Maybe Sam isn't there yet."

"It is rather early there, at least an hour earlier there, I think, so let's enjoy our breakfast. Do you have anything else to add?" He pointed to the list.

Pidalios chewed and read, then said, "Yes, you know I keep thinking about Dr. Karis and how he behaved toward you and John at the autopsy. It was so unusual for him to be so uncooperative. Maybe we should look into that."

"I thought he was just in a bad mood, but it's worth trying to talk to him. Let's go to Kaminia first. We can check with the good doctor later, and, if I don't call your Thia to see if she wants to come, there will be hell to pay. All right with you?"

"I'll even let her sit up front next to me," he laughed.

Irini was standing at the curb outside the apartment. She was holding a box of glika for Mavrogenis. Pidalios leaned across the seat and opened the door for her. "Thia, ride up here with me."

She got in, said good morning and reached back to squeeze her husband's hand. "I don't know if we will see Kyrios Mavrogenis, but I walked around the corner and got some sweets for him, just in case."

"You mean they're not payment for the driver?" her nephew said.

From the back seat Geró said, Salman Rushdie, the author, wrote, "'In the cookie of life, relatives are chocolate chips.' I think he actually said friends, but in your case you must earn your chips." He gave a hearty laugh as he patted his nephew's shoulder.

Irini just rolled her eyes in the mirror. The two explained to her why they were going back to Kaminia. She might be able to have a chat with the old man while they had a second look in the house. Luckily, Mavrogenis was sitting on his porch and waved as they drove up. With a gesture he pooh-poohed Irini's apology for just arriving. He thanked her for the treat plus the copy of her last book.

Pidalios and Geró left her there and drove on to the Katsouris house. Once again they had easy access and searched the harmoukela in its entirety of one large room and fireplace. Other than years of accumulated cob webs and dirt, they found nothing except for a tiny piece of red shredded fabric stuck on a stone. Pidalios bagged and tagged it. Then they went outside and walked through the overgrown weeds and growth—finding nothing. They were walking back to the car and met a woman who questioned their presence. She told them she had seen a woman there, and, when asked for possible identification of that woman, all she could offer was that her hair was dark. Geró's thought was 'like so many Greek women.'

When they went back to pick up Irini, she was engrossed in what Mavrogenis was telling her. He licked his sticky fingers and said, "You brought me two pleasures this morning: a conversation with your wife and some of the best Melomakarona I have ever tasted. She tells me these are her favorite cookies too."

"Kyrios Mavrogenis has been telling me stories about this village—stories from way back." She turned to smile at the old man. "I was particularly caught by the one about the German officer who pretended to be sympathetic to the villagers but then ordered the shooting of several leaders here in the village." She leaned back and cast her eyes down.

"I will try to relate happier references to our history next time, and thank you for this book. I will check with others here, detectives, if they know anything else about the Katsouris family, and if they might know what happened to Maria after she was vilified by rumor and gossip all those years ago."

As they drove away, Irini said, "That man is a delight, and thanks to you two for bringing me along. It was so worthwhile to sit with such a wise man. Let me explain it like this. I saw a film, entitled, 'Smilla's Feeling for Snow.' A line from it that stays with me is: 'Some thoughts have glue on them.' Do you understand?"

"That's why you enjoy talking with us, Thia." Pidalios turned the wheel and drove out of Kaminia.

Chapter 19

With a promise to be home at a reasonable hour, Geró said goodbye to Irini outside their apartment building. He and Pidalios decided to stop off at the hospital on the chance that Dr. Karis might be there. He wasn't. His resident, Dr. Veloutis, the pleasant man they dealt with before, said that Karis just left for home.

"It's early for απογεματινό υπνάκο [apogematino eep nako-afternoon snooze]. Can we call him there?" asked Pidalios.

"No, I'm sorry. He does not want to be disturbed by anyone," Veloutis said as he tried to sound firm.

"You do remember me: the detective who was present at the autopsy?"

"Certainly I do. You're Γερό Πυρούνι."

"What time will he return this evening?"

"He won't. He told me before noon, the day after tomorrow."

"What if there's an emergency?"

"His instructions were that I or another doctor could handle it. Look, I'm sure you need to talk to Dr. Karis, but I can't help you."

Pidalios spoke up. "We have known the doctor for some time, and there seems to be a change in his manner—very abrupt. Are you aware of it? Is he all right? We're only asking because he seems so different."

"To everyone, but I don't have the right to ask anything other than, 'How are you, doctor?' He just says, 'fine' and does not offer anything further. I will tell him you came to see him. Why not call in a day or two."

"He's not ill or anything?"

"Doesn't seem to be, but he does not share personal news with me or the staff."

Geró said, "We'll check again. Thank you, doctor." They left. In the car he asked, "How old do you think Dr. Karis is?"

"Why? Do you think he is losing it?"

"No, I am wondering though. Find out his age and where he was raised, family connections, wife, background…"

"…In other words I am supposed to simply check on his entire life."

"Well, you're the one who is so great on instant information and data."

"You mean my cell phone? Look, Thio, I'll check the library's microfilm. I'll ask around about his relatives, family and wherever else I can check. You said you were going to call Sam. I'll drop you at the office."

Geró looked at the dashboard clock. It would be 11 a.m. in Cairo. He could call his old friend now at Egypt's SSI (State Security Investigations). It was the office of the central security and intelligence apparatus of Egypt's Ministry of Interior. His friend 'Sam,' whose real name was Fouad Samaha, had given him the extension number. Sam had been an agent at SSI for years and was referred to by his code name Sam, not because of secrecy or undercover stuff. Many outsiders had trouble pronouncing Fouad correctly. He grew tired of being called Fau-wood, Foul-ood and other such laughable monikers, so he chose the name Sam from his last name, Samaha. Even his charming wife Litza, who happened to be Greek, called him Sam, when she wasn't using Fouad in formal settings.

"SSI," said the man answering the phone.

"My name is Geró Peerooney, from Sparta, Greece. I am a personal friend of Sam. I wish to speak with him."

"Please give me your phone number there, and you will be contacted."

Geró knew better than to argue with a bureaucratic clerk, so he obliged and hung up. Within a half hour his phone rang with a response.

"Hello, sir. Am I speaking to Geró?"

"That's correct. And you are?"

"Tarek Scharaff. I am calling from SSI, our Interpol. I am Sam's nephew, and it is a pleasure to speak with you."

Geró knew the name of the caller because Sam had bragged about his nephew, an agent at SSI. Tarek was a son of an important man who had been Egypt's ambassador to several countries, and Tarek proudly carried on the family name.

"I understand that you called to speak to my uncle, sir, but he is not here."

"I hope he is well and has not retired or...."

"Him? no, but he is closer to you at this time. He is in Athens. May I do something for you, or get a message to him?"

"I appreciate the offer, and I thank you. Can you possibly fax me his number so I can call him, or can he reach me?"

"This is a secure phone, and it would be better if I have him call you, sir. I know he would be delighted to speak with his old friend."

Geró knew his number would be safe with Tarek, so he gave it as well as Pidalios' cell number to him after he explained who his nephew was. Then he told Tarek Scharaff that he would like to greet him in person one day.

"If you are ever in Cairo…."

"I thank you and extend the same invitation to you. Ma'assalama, Tarek."

"I only wish I knew how to say 'goodbye with peace and safety' in Greek. Thank you," and he ended the call.

What an agreeable man, thought Geró. He waited less than an hour before his phone rang. "Detective agency."

"Very businesslike, old friend."

"Fouad, I'd know that voice anywhere. How are you?"

"Just fine, but wondering how you are. It's been what six years?"

"That's correct, and we're both still in the business."

They went on to discuss family, health, the world, and two friends reunited on the phone. "I am working, still with my nephew, on a case: murder on a wild boar hunt here up on Tayegatos. My friend, John Sakalidis, captain of the Astynomia, asked us to consult."

He waited for an interrupting question from 'Sam,' but the man just listened. Geró remembered a quote from a Canadian, David Tyson. 'True friendship comes when the silence between two people is comfortable.' He continued to explain the circumstances of the killing, and how they had first believed that Fotis Grigoris (formerly Grigorakis) was the suspect until now. At this time they were concentrating on a woman—Maria Katsouris from the 1941 incident. He said that she had disappeared from Kaminia after the shooting of a married man and after her public shaming.

Then rumor had it that she went to Athens to fight with the partisans. If alive, she would be about seventy years old now.

"Since you have Interpol connections, and Tarek told me you are in Athens—by the way I was very impressed with him—good man. I do want to see you, if possible. Can I meet you there, or wherever you wish? Maybe you can give me any information you find about Maria Katsouris."

"First, thank you for recognizing the worth of my nephew. He is a very honorable man. I am here snooping around for other reasons, but I can connect with this Intel division to search for your woman. Obviously, this is of paramount importance to you. Let me see, it's Wednesday. I will need a few days and we'll meet. And bring your wife; it is still Irini?"

"Who else?"

"I will bring Litza. I have the use of an agency house in Gytheio, fairly close to you, yes?"

"Perfect, we love Gytheio."

"We can enjoy good food (maybe barbouni from the Gulf) and talk. Our wives will enjoy their reunion also. We can be there Saturday if I find out anything. Otherwise I'll call to postpone."

"I understand. Irini is a good driver, and she will be happy to see you both."

"You don't drive?"

"That's a story for another time."

"Then don't you want to include your partner?"

"Yes, and I'll wait for your call. I owe you for this, my friend."

They had met in Athens when Geró was still an Astynomia detective, and Fouad Samaha was moving up fast in Interpol. They got along so well that they and their wives met for dinner in Vouliagmeni and other scenic spots around the area. They looked forward to these dinners and how relaxed two Greeks, an Egyptian and an American were in shared friendship.

Friday afternoon Sam called to say that he had something, though maybe not enough to help them. They agreed to meet in Gytheio at 7 p.m. on Saturday in front of the city hall on the promenade. They should follow his car, a plain gray Audi, up to the 'villa.' He also said Litza sent her love and was looking forward to the evening.

****

They did not get out of the cars. Pidalios followed the Audi up the steep climb to a house in a wooded off-road area overlooking the harbor. Irini went to Litza and hugged her. "I saw you through the car window, when I waved, and said to Geró and Pidalios, 'I'd know Litza anywhere. Her lovely face is still crowned with natural, shining silver hair. I envy her."

"Thank you, and it's wonderful to see you again, dear Irini. I won't compliment you too much now, otherwise you will think I don't mean it." She smiled.

Hugs, handshakes feelakia (kisses) were freely given by all, and Litza mused over how thoughtfully Irini had included Pidalios' name when she repeated what she said in the car. She always thought of everyone; no one would be embarrassed by a forgotten name.

The five made the most of those few hours. The locally caught barbouni was delicious, and conversation was easy. They sat on the open balcony, constructed entirely of stones and arches to enable appreciation of the mountainside and bay panorama from the side of Mt. Koumaros.

Irini and Litza decided an after dinner stroll was in order, and the three men settled in so 'Sam' could tell them what he found about Maria Katsouris. Geró didn't expect much information, yet he was pleased with what they learned. They were handed a print copy of her ancestry.

Maria Katsouris, a fifteen year old girl from Kaminia in 1941, left her village and fled. She made her way to Athens. She had no means of support. She joined the underground and fought under the code name "Sorceress." Her time with the partisans turned her into a fierce communist. When the civil war in Greece ended, she couldn't go home, so she stayed in Athens and married a fellow partisan, a man of some means. Their only child, a girl, was also named Maria because of the father's mother.

Tradition rules, you know, even among communists.

"Young Maria—married name Tsouros now—learned to handle arms very well. She was a member of a militaristic, communist family and went hunting with her husband in the Balkans."

He showed them a picture from Interpol's file, a photo of a commie hunting party at a winter lodge. In the picture was Maria Tsouros taken several years ago.

Pidalios said, "short, petite, dark hair. That could be the woman the chopanis saw. Can we keep this picture?"

"I brought enlarged prints for all who are working on this murder," said Sam. "I also found that our original Maria, Katouris that is, passed away on October 1, this year, of 'natural causes.' The woman was a virago, bitter from her life's tragedy in Kaminia all those years before."

"Her daughter must have lived with her mother's turbulence and anger. People can't keep things like that private, not when it completely turned her life upside down," Geró noted. "Is she still living with her husband?"

"That I did not check on."

"Leaves something for me to find out," quipped Pidalios, which brought laughter.

They said goodbye with promises to get together. Geró thanked 'Sam' for everything he had found and said he would keep his friend, now very interested, informed. There was no need to follow the gray Audi now, and Pidalios' car pulled away quite slowly from the house.

Chapter 20

"I took a quick trip to Kaminia from Anogia when I got up this morning," Pidalios reported as he entered the office. He was still chewing his fried bread and held an iced coffee. "Sorry," he pointed to his mouth. I didn't stop in Sparta because I was so hungry."

"Don't apologize. I made coffee, and I don't want to get into the fried bread habit— too hard to break and still keep this body." He winked. "Did you find out anything?"

"Dr. Karis' wife, Sula is her name, was born in Kaminia. She's sixty-eight years old— older than the doctor by five years."

"Go on."

"She was a close friend of the original Maria when they were young girls, that is until Maria got a bum rap and ran away."

"Why do you say bum rap?"

"That's the talk of some old people, my new friends, in that horio."

"They say that now, but it's the usual gossip—probably to keep you involved in their conversation. And you're cute and respectful. Did you find Mrs. Karis?"

"No. They don't live in Kaminia any longer. They live somewhere in one of those really nice houses in Magoula."

"What's the address?"

"Who knows."

"We'll ask the doctor when we see him. Maybe he'll talk a bit more. Let's stop in again on Wednesday; he should be back by then."

"In the meantime I'm going to the library to do some more detective work. I'll be gone a few hours probably. I've got to watch microfilm, check history books about our civil war, the underground, and see what other resources are available. My cell phone will be on silent, so if you need me, walk over and quietly pinch my shoulder hard. I may have fallen asleep."

Geró smiled at his nephew's retreating back. He was a good detective now, one who would do any task or go anywhere to get to the truth—albeit complaining all the while. It was always done though with good humor. He yelled after him, "'Stay away from negative people. They have a problem for every solution.'"

"Who said that?" Pidalios screamed up from the stairwell as he descended.

"Damned if I know." Geró knew that during this quiet time he also would be able to work. He began to make a handwritten chart on erasable white board. He printed 'what we know' as one column heading and 'people involved' on another. How clear it became on the boards.

In his mind he could hear Irini saying, 'Not just the phone number; put the name down too. Otherwise you just have all those scraps of paper in that rubber band you carry.' She was right again!

First he wrote the names of the shooter and the victim. Their family trees and important dates were next, then village connections, chopanis' statements and evidence. He had filled two boards when Capt. Sakalidis called. "Geró, I hope you're not with anyone, but I just had an interesting call from Brussels. A perfume maker/distributor called me because I am the police captain, and he told me that information on a customer had been requested by someone at Interpol. He did not have your name, so he called me here."

"Yes, I think he wanted to talk to me. We have that match on the hair clump, found up on Tayegatos and on an old blanket at the abandoned Katsouris house. Probably my friend Sam is behind this."

Well, he said the perfume matches one brand, Pani Walewska, originally made by Miraculum. It was first blended in Paris in the 30s, but it is no longer as popular—very heavy scent—and is quite expensive, so their customer list has dwindled. One customer, their only Greek, don't laugh now, orders under the name 'Sorceress.' He told me it was last purchased by her on their website about one year ago—nothing since then."

"John, this is terrific! My source told me that her code name, when she fought with the underground, was Sorceress, and she fought 'to wave the bloody shirt,' as the saying goes. It is definitely Maria Katsouris, who died on October 1 to be exact in Athens.

"I have to add that there is so much going on in the study of odorology now. Irini did the research, and that's how I heard of this. I must give her credit. It could help with clues in the future."

"If Katsouris died on October 1, how did the scented hair and blanket end up in Kaminia in November?" John asked.

"She has a daughter who uses the same name, Greek citizen."

"Like mother, like daughter, maybe?"

"We'll see, but thanks for this, my friend."

"Glad to help." He hung up.

Geró was so pleased by this connection that he walked the six cracked-sidewalk streets to the library to tell Pidalios.

"Ouch!"

"You said to pinch you."

"My shoulder, not my neck."

"Never mind that," said his uncle as he sat down. "John Sakalidis just called. His news is that a Greek woman, whose account is under the name Sorceress, orders the same scent we have identified from a perfume distributor in

Brussels. It was last ordered a year ago, and it was sent to an address in Athens."

"Did he get that address?"

"The man said he was not at liberty to…you know the usual skata [shit]."

"We'll get it."

"Good, keep at it," Geró patted his head and left.

When Pidalios went back to the office later, he admired the white boards and gave his own report. "I researched all the possible phone and address information sites, such as: XO,gr, the OTE phone book, vrisko local search [vrisko.gr]. Her number must be disconnected or unlisted. Don't be discouraged; I have other methods."

****

Wednesday morning, after calling first, Geró and Pidalios entered Dr. Karis' office at the hospital to be greeted by an inquisitive look on Karis' face: "I thought I gave you all the information I had after the autopsy on Vrasithas Politis."

"Scant at best," replied Geró. We came before to ask you a few questions but were told you were gone and would not be back for several days. Were you ill or on vacation?"

"Hardly. My wife and I drove to Athens to attend a forty day memorial service to remember her friend she has kept in touch with for years."

"Sorry to hear that. Your wife Sula, right?"

"Yes."

"This friend? Was her name Maria Katsouris?"

"Why do you ask? Because she fought with the underground so many years ago, and once a cop always a cop?"

"No, because she may have been connected to the same murder we're investigating."

"Not possible. She died October 1. The shooting was opening day of hunting season, November 1." He smirked at them after that gotcha remark.

"What we need from you now is her home address."

"I can give you that. It's Othos Paraskevis in the Peristeri section of Athens—nice area.

She lived there for years, even stayed after she was widowed."

Pidalios asked, "Was her daughter, also Maria, there?"

"Not that I saw, but I wouldn't know her anyway. Someone said she had a daughter, who was at the funeral, but could not bear to attend the memorial."

"Does she live in her mother's house?" Karis just shrugged.

"Doctor, are you aware that the man who allegedly shot Politis is the grandson of the 'sheriff' who shot Politis—that's the 1941 Politis?" Geró asked.

"How would I know that?"

"Your wife never mentioned how her friend was shamed in that incident. Supposedly she was the one who had a tryst with that Vrasithas Politis, and then she went on to fight with the underground and become a fierce communist?"

"Look, many Greeks joined or were sympathetic to communism, but I had nothing to do with my wife's childhood friend. I only know that she was involved in a scandal in

Kaminia, through no fault of her own, and fled to Athens. Sula periodically kept in touch by phone or mail and, when she heard of the death, she persuaded me to at least go to the memorial service. We went to the church and stayed only an hour at the luncheon. Sula hardly knew anyone there."

"Your address, doctor? In case we need to ask your wife about Maria Katsouris."

He grudgingly gave it with a warning not to harass them, and finished by saying, "Now, if you need anything else concerning the post mortem on Politis, ask Dr. Veloutis. He can help you." He was already reaching for his cigarettes as he preceded them out the door.

Chapter 21

"Geró, I did a little more research, but only on Google today. You know that perfume Pani Walewska I told you about?" Irini said.

"Did you talk to John today?" He cut her off.

"John who?" She sounded irritated.

"Sakalidis. Why do you always ask 'who?' after I say a name?"

"Because all Greek men, probably self-importance rearing its ugly head again, never say a last name. We must know at least twenty Johns, and how am I supposed to guess which one you're referring to, and, no, I didn't speak to that particular John."

He ignored his wife's cut and filled her in on his conversation with the captain, and he used John's last name.

"I was going to tell you that Pani means madam in Polish and Slovak. The perfume was named for Maria Walewska, a woman Napoleon fell desperately in love with. The perfume was very popular in Poland and Russia," Irini reported.

"Maybe that's why this Maria wore it, and now, thanks to you, I have learned the meaning of 'Pani,' and I will try to use last names in the future."

She ignored the sarcasm and responded, "You know, Gerómou, what I keep thinking about? The red bow that you found tied to the bush up on Tayegatos—did that have any significance, or did it just blow in on the wind?"

"It is definitely connected. The bow was artfully tied. The evidence on it of a fingerprint in gun oil is still at the lab. We did find a scrap from the same ribbon in the fireplace at the hamoukela in Kaminia. The edge showed what looked like dried blood. Also, there is a small amount of soil with some blood evidence. All of that is in Thodoris and Taki's possession at the moment."

"What's the motive for the murder? Is it hatred of Politis? revenge?" she asked, "but for what? He never caused any tragedy, or ruined any life."

"We'll find that out when the case is solved. My only thought is that the life of her mother Maria was totally changed by an unproven accusation against her. Supposedly, she became a termagant, a fierce fighter, an angry woman."

"How odd that she wore Pani Walewska perfume."

"But it is a cloying, heavy scent, you said."

****

The captain held a meeting in his office. Around the table were Geró, Pidalios, Sgt. Goovis, Officer Vatis. Taking part via conference call were Thodoris and Taki. They had earlier made a private call to the detective agency to thank Geró and Pidalios for the 'gift' promised from them. In that package, delivered to the lab, they found equipment: an inclinometer, a digital directional compass and a laser pointer. The gift tag said only: "When 'Stringing,' you will no longer need string."

"I think we have evidence on the possible murderer of Vrasithas Politis," said Sakalidis as he stood by the big board on the easel. "First, let's make it clear that Fotis Grigoris

[Grigorakis] did not kill him because the slug from his gun did not enter the deceased's body. It was discharged when he tripped on the roots while walking behind. It was found ahead of the body.

"Our other suspect is a woman, Maria Katsouris. If she is still married, you can add the surname Tsouros. We think she lives in Peristeri, in Athens.

"I called all of you together for this meeting because you play either a major role in the solution, or you have somehow been involved with questioning or collecting data, either at the crime scene, in Kaminia, or at our lab in Tripoli, and the Astynomia thanks you for your work. Maybe we will finally get an answer for Politis' widow and children."

Each of those present and on the call now spoke or handed in their results. "The lab matched the DNA in the tattered blanket with the blood in the soil and on the scrap of ribbon in the fireplace. These days we are able to analyze minute samples. It is referred to as low level DNA or 'Touch DNA.'"

"Is it true you can get it even from a textured surface, such as a gun handle or a car dashboard?" Geró questioned.

"Absolutely true, but still the best evidence is found where it isn't supposed to be. For instance, there is a break in at a home. Later maybe a glove is found outside the house. The home owner says, 'It's not mine,' and hairs from the perpetrator's hand are found inside that glove. They are used for a DNA test to prove his crime."

"I'm curious, since I bagged the soil containing blood, how the specimen got in the dirt," asked Pidalios.

"Taki said, "Since it was also on the bow and ribbon fabric, she probably slit her finger while tying it—you know, like a paper cut, and how long that can take to stop bleeding. That's my guess."

The captain asked, "The saliva on the foil pack in the Fisherman's Friend box—that was also a match?"

"Yes, it was, as was the dark hair caught on the bush up there. We even got a hair root and tissue match with the blanket from the hamoukela," said Taki, but it does not match any criminal database."

"Why would a murderer take the time to tie a bow to a limb at the scene, and why the color red? I'd like to know that," said Toula Vatis. "Is it a symbol?"

"You will ask her when she is arrested, won't you?" Sgt. Goovis asked. "Also, did Dr. Karis' autopsy agree with all the findings?"

"We have his agreement, and he finally concurred on the angle of entry of the shot," said Pidalios. "While we have them on the line, "I would like to give praise to everyone, especially Thodoris and Taki, who took part in the 'Stringing Test' to prove that angle." Talking stopped as the lab men received the applause of all in the room.

"Geró, you and Pidalios took the case, when the department needed you; as is usual, you had the wherewithal to solve it. What other thoughts or questions are there?"

"We have two chopanithes who helped us, and Tsengos actually saw the woman up there and saw her run away when he called out to her. She had a large black bag with her. Maybe it held the gun. We have to find out how she got rid of it—buried it or threw it somewhere?"

Pidalios added, "John, we have the toxicological reports, witnesses and, if her shoe size matches the cast, we need to find and interrogate her."

"Geró said, "John, we think she might be in her mother's house in Peristeri, on Othos Paraskevis [Paraskevis Street]...."

"I will contact our people in Athens. They can do a stakeout on the house to see if she comes and goes. I'll call after this meeting."

"Thank you all for helping my partner and me." Everyone exchanged congratulatory pats on backs while offering any further help needed. They left and John promised to get back to his consultants with the results of the stakeout.

It was only a few days later when the captain called Geró at home in the evening. Irini answered the phone, exchanged pleasantries with him and said, "Just a moment; he's nearby. She called her husband, "Geró, it's John."

Her husband, who held his hand over the phone, said to her, "You only called him John." She punched him softly, and he said, "Good evening, John."

"Geró, the stakeout worked. It is Othos Paraskevis 28 in Peristeri. The officers described only one resident emerging and returning to that house over a two day period. It is a small woman with long, dark hair, and it sounds like our suspect. We arranged to have her picked up and brought in for questioning later in the day tomorrow."

"You're the best, John. What's the plan?"

"I have to go, so I'll drive you and Pidalios. Let's leave my office at 9, so we will easily be there before noon, and bring your files."

"With pleasure."

"Since it happened in our jurisdiction, if she is arrested by us, we'll arrange to have her brought here. See you in the morning."

The three men entered the Astynomia precinct in Athens right after noon and were ushered to the commander's office for a meeting. Of course, metrio coffee [Greek coffee] was ordered from the kafenion next door. The Spartans were told that the officers called and said they had a feisty Maria Katsouris in their car and would be arriving shortly.

Their entrance was announced by the voice of a vocal and angry woman. She was then seated at a table in a gray, cement block room, and an officer stood watch over her. The door opened and Capt. John Sakalidis, Geró and Pidalios entered, introduced themselves, sat and after ignoring her outraged protests, began to question her. It was explained that she was a person of interest in the death by shotgun of one Vrasithas Politis from Kaminia. She did not wait for the first question before she blurted out, "I never heard of him, and what right do you have to bring a total stranger to a police station without a warrant or an explanation first?"

"We are trying to explain right now if you will let us. Is a warrant for your arrest necessary at the beginning of these simple questions? If so, we can get one," said the commander of the precinct, who had come in.

"These men have driven two hours to get information. Why don't you cooperate and make it easier on yourself."

The short, dark-haired woman sat bolt upright in the chair, seemingly struggling to adjust her body comfortably in the chair. She said nothing.

"Your name is Maria Tsouros, nee Katsouris, is it not?"

"Skip the Tsouros; he's gone." She was curt.

"Was your mother's name also Maria?"

Her knuckles whitened, grasping the arms of the chair. "Leave my mother out of this. She's dead."

"We are aware of that," said the captain "and extend condolences, but your mother's life plays a large part in our information. Her name was also Maria—Maria Katsouris, and we find that she and you were…are registered members of the communist party in Greece, and your mother fought in the underground and resistance after she left Kaminia. Is that not true?"

"Look at this! You drag me here to ask if I'm a communist. I can't believe you fools."

Geró said, "No, that's not the only reason. If you can't calm down and answer, we'll be here until tomorrow. Please respond to Captain Sakalidis."

"Yes, all right, it's true," she snapped at them.

"Why did she continue to use the surname Katsouris, even after she was married? Frankly, you choose the same path, don't you?"

"She never wanted anyone in Kaminis to forget her name and what that 'sheriff' Grigorakis and his bullies did to ruin her life. Well, at least he got his." She smirked.

"But that was so many years ago—1941. This is almost 1996. Didn't she ever get over the obvious wrong done to her by him and the gossip mob in the village?"

"How would you feel if it happened to your fifteen year old, innocent daughter, captain, and she had no one to go to, no money and was being falsely accused of the worst thing for a girl in those times. She was destroyed, no future, no husband to fight for her, no place to run." She settled back in her chair. Her teeth were still gritted. "Her only choices were prostitution in some city or what she did do. Her mother might have been sympathetic, but her father was a hard ass, and men ruled.

"It is obvious to me that you lived with the fury suffered by your mother," said Pidalios.

"Thank the gods of Olympus that she made it to Athens. You know, all of you upstanding men, the only help she got was acceptance by the underground. She learned to be tough, a fierce fighter. My father, also in the underground, a believer in that ideology, gave her a home…"

"and you were born," said Pidalios.

She burst with hysterical laughter. "That wasn't so great for her or me. Sure she had a place to stay and money if she wanted to buy something…"

"…like expensive Pani Walewska perfume?" asked Geró.

She looked startled by their depth of information but got hold of herself to say,

"Sure, it suited her, and I would borrow it too, without asking. My father gave her things, but he had no time for her. He gave the little love he could, but more money than love."

"Were you close to her?"

"Let's say we bonded over the same emotion—anger fueled by hatred. She was obsessed and passed her fury on to me." Maria realized she had unleashed too much of herself: a catharsis of all she had kept bottled up all these years, and she abruptly stopped talking.

"What was the purpose of the red bow?"

"Red bow?"

"You know all about it. Was there a reason for it?"

"You mean the red bows my mother always wore...on her neck, in her hair?" Their murderer was falling back into 'telling on' her mother.

"Only her hair and neck?" asked Geró.

"She loved red. I think she always thought she was still 'waving the bloody shirt.' She once wore a peppery red damask gown to a party event in Athens."

"A bit overdressed, wasn't she?" Pidalios asked. "Ah, it was a RED event though."

"She was the 'Sorceress.'"

"You didn't like your mother very much," said Pidalios.

"I LOVED my mother!" she shrieked.

The officer on duty moved closer to her chair. The commander waved him off.

"That's why I took such care in tying that bow."

"The bow on the top of the hill?"

She ignored that and said, "I picked the satiny ribbon especially for her. Before she died, I promised her I would get revenge. If it weren't for him, she might have had a happy life and in her own horio. So, I took my hunting rifle, and on November 1st, the season opener;

I hunt, you know. I was told by a villager that they were going after wild boar up there…"

"…who said it?"asked the captain.

"So you can arrest her too? I went to our house the night before and tied the most beautiful bow for my mother."

"Where? the house in Kaminia?" asked Geró.

As if he hadn't asked, she continued, "It's a long walk from there to my position up on the mountain. I had worn my best hunting boots."

"Your feet are very small."

The now obviously deranged woman, smiled and bragged, "size 36 or 6 in America," as she lifted one foot to show them. I was ready, had all my equipment, put my hood up and my ασφάλεια [as fal eia—security bag] and hiked up there. After observing them, I prepared my spot above them." She was bragging in the telling.

Capt. Sakalidis said, " Did you realize you were about to commit a murder?"

She laughed as she brazenly threw her head back. "Murder? Are you serious? It was payback for all he and his relative had caused her and me."

Geró's thought at that moment was that he was observing the embodiment of a mythomaniac. She believed her own fantasy, and he said aloud, "'…and it is not right to return an injury, or do evil to any man, however much we have suffered from him.' Think about the truth in Socrates' words, Maria."

"All that is important to me, old man, is that like my mother I had to accomplish my mission."

Sakalidis knew they were dealing with an unrepentant killer, so he said, "Let's get back to the scene. What did you do with your gun afterward?"

"That was easy. I put it in the big bag after the chopanis yelled to me, ran away from him and took the ferry from Gytheion to Crete. Halfway there I strolled to the far end of the deck and threw the entire bag into the water." She smiled very smugly. "No one saw me."

All in the room just looked at each other, and Captain John Sakalidis took the lead. "Maria Katsouris, I am placing you under arrest for the murder of Vrasithas Politis on November 1, 1995. We will now go to fingerprints and photography."

She began to laugh hysterically. "Μαλάκες [malakes—assholes], I was aiming for the pig,

Fotis Grigorakis [Grigoris], but my foot slipped, and I ended up killing the other guy! The joke is on you."

They led her away to be booked.

Maria Katsouris was tried, convicted, and her sentence for killing the wrong man was sixteen to twenty years in prison. On November 1, 1996, she committed suicide by hanging herself. She had a red bow in her hair.

••

"The old man used to say that the best part of hunting and fishing was thinking about it going and talking about it after you got back."

Robert Ruark
(The Old Man and the Boy 1957)

Acknowledgments

Ilias Konstantakakos, a friend from Sparta, Greece, listened as I explained the plot for my next book: A man accidentally? shoots a friend in the back during their wild boar hunt. Ilias told me that many years before his godfather had threatened a malefactor, accused of an 'evil' deed. Then he shot that man with his pistola.

I changed the characters, the motive, the demeanor of those involved so that the story is totally fictitious, and this book is the result.

Thank you, Ilias.

Enid Newman, friend, who gives her talent, support and much of her time to book layout, cover design and fixing my screw ups while offering the best suggestions. Her daughter, Lauren Alter, also helped to fix the formatting errors that were found along the way.

Louis Soumakis, my Geró and real life husband, who supports me and brags about my novels to all who cross his path.

Judith Gifford, friend, who supports and encourages and crafts title cards for me.

Fouad and Litza Samaha for research information, friendship and permission to use their real names.

Panagiotis Economopoulos, nephew, who patiently corrects to my Greek, explains the Greece I still do not know and tolerates my constant questions.

Harry Brown Cook IV, friend and brother, for his loyal support.

Margaret and Harry Brown Cook III, dear parents and Geraldine Romano, sister---just because.

Norena Soumakis, the author of this and five other novels, is a former English teacher on Long Island, New York , where she lives with her husband, Louis, when they are not at home in Greece.